The Short St
Poems and Proses

BY
Noreen W S Song

WITH ILLUSTRATIONS BY
Noreen W S Song

To my MUM and DAD,
who love me, always support me, and let me. choose
my path

And…

Thanks to Aunt Doris
Whether it's guiding me to fall in love with
reading or choosing Cottesmore school (a school,
which has significantly influenced me)

For Mr. Rogerson,
who cared about Cottesmore School,
and for all the teachers who taught me there.

Preface

I love reading before I go to bed. But if I'm at home on exeat or the other term holidays, and if my mom doesn't urge or hush me to sleep, I can lose track of time reading a book and become so sleepy that I didn't know when I fell asleep! Please don't copy me - this is not a good habit for children! I often get inspiration and fabulous ideas when I'm reading. This is why I can never wait to write a story, and that's why I have so many short stories in this collection.

As I am a whole boarder at Cottesmore the school will turn off the dormitory lights at 8:30pm.

I started writing stories when I was eight years old. I finished this collection when I was ten. A short story collection means that reader has more options – if you find one story boring, maybe the next one will help you lose track of time, like I do. Reading books can power up your vocabulary and your English. If you decide to write like me – never give up. One day you could also become an author. So, remember, NEVER GIVE UP!

CONTENTS

Short Stories:

Poems:

1. The odd mushroom
2. The king parrots
3. The jelly sections
4. The Beauty of White
5. Hop Hop Hop
6. Bloom it!
7. The striped cat
8. The special almond tarts
9. The yellowish rattlesnake
10. On the way home
11. Super Mum
12. Super-Duper Daddy
13. My family
14. Monsters
15. Every Flower's life
16. My family II
17. The Christmas
18. Everything
19. The Summer Holiday
20. For Saka, Rashford, and Sancho
21. The world
22. Lego
23. A journey on the train
24. Fruit
25. The seasons (the haiku type which only has three lines)

Essays:

1. The star of the Spring
2. The searing of Summer
   Part I – Cool summer days at the beach
   Part II – The blistering summer of June and July
   Part III – The hot air will solidify
   Part IIII – Beautiful coastline in summer
3. The Autumn
4. The Winter's Tale
5. The wonderful Tilgate park
6. The race of nature
7. The Meadow, the plain, and the forest

Story 1

M innelli's Flower shop!

Minnelli was the daughter of a low-income family; you probably know that because they only had 5p or even a halfpenny each! The family didn't have even one pound, and they were poor!

So, one day Minnelli was going to cut some trees to build a shed for her family. She went on a path that leads to Flower Forest, and shouted, "Yay!", in her most excited voice. Seeing the glory of light through the trees, Minnelli ran towards the forest.

She took off her backpack and took an axe out. She cut herself an unusual large flower tree, which even more unusually, didn't weigh anything. She thought that if she opened a flower shop with such a strange flower tree, it would attract many curious people and would help her earn a great income. She imagined the possibilities of it all and felt obliged to begin her project at once.

As soon as she arrived back at her house, she put the gigantic flower tree into the little garden.

A month later, and after rebuilding her parents' house, she built a glass hut which would become a flower shop. She planted the flower tree inside the hut, and it fitted perfectly! She then built a fence around the hut and hung a wooden sign, Minnelli's Flower Shop, at the entrance.

Just as she had imagined, the enormous flowers on the tree attracted many customers. She was as busy as a bee! She then built a shelf onto the wall to hold a watering can and a robot. To earn extra pocket money and pay for the robot she also sold some lemonade in the shop. She was proud of herself. Minnelli then bought some accessories like pottery and stuff, but these were not for selling!

After two weeks Minnelli had enough money to afford to go to school. She had saved £3,600. She decided to give £125 to charity and use the remainder to help with her schooling and for other people in need.

Several years later when Minnelli was going back to visit her childhood home near the flower forest, she saw a pig-sized, humongous bee sucking some nectar from a flower. She enjoyed watching the bee so much, she decided to put it into an empty glass tank.

From then on, she cared for the bee by throwing in some flowers from her flower tree. Minnelli not only had loads of money, but she also now had loads of honey.

Story 2

S ummery camp with my friends in the UK

Ok, so I'm Daisy. And Urticaria is my friend. She is my best friend ever and was the oldest of her siblings. We called her Una for short. Marina was her friend. Wendy was also our friend. She was the youngest of all of us and she was also the most knowledgeable. Our other friend Andy wasn't the smartest. We all began summer camp in the UK together…

"Mrs. Keane, can I please take Urticaria to summer camp? It's full of discos and other stuff," I asked.

"Especially practice exams, and it might include several field trips or special occasions."

"Yes," replied Mrs Keane, "but only if you let her wear summer dresses as it is to be a scorching day. Take thicker clothes to keep her warm, if needed."

Names	Age	Smart?	Abnormal?
Urticaria	8	Yes, very	No
Marina	8	Yes, but not very	No
Wendy	7yrs 11mths	Yes, super!	Nope
Andy	8		Neither

"Thanks," I said.

One by one I asked all my friends if they would come with me to the camp. I then told my parents about what would happen in the next few days, and my mum was very excited about it.

The precious day came at last. My friends and I gathered at the gate for an airport called Gatwick. They just laughed at the name for no reason!

An hour later and we were on the plane, and you know, I just loved the way my friends smiled. We arrived in the UK and, 12 hours after first leaving, we were in our hotel room. The hotel was close to a beautiful beach, and we could watch the sunbathers.

I could go to the beach in Spain even though it's a long way from the hotel. I did find a little wooden hut with nothing in it but a pile of sand. It's a place where even beach chairs and umbrellas are a luxury. But in the hut I found a chest that wasn't locked, and guess what I saw in it? £500 pounds! Woweee!

"Darling! Well done! Finally, I can pay for the summer camp," said Mum loudly, so that everybody could hear what she was talking about at the great grand table in the dining room that the hotel has.

Story 3

M elody Curve's Story of Sport

"Good morning, darling!" said Melody's mom. "Cuddle?" Melody responded.

Off Melody went downstairs to prepare her breakfast. She brushed her hair, brushed her teeth, and washed her face with face cream. Her mom gave her a lunchbox for school just before the school bus arrived. She just made it in time!

At school, something unique happened.

"Hello, students!", called the sports teacher. The teacher then checked if any of his students are missing. "Layla? Tom? Eva? Lucas? Oscar?", asked the sports teacher.

"Yes, sir!", they all replied.

"Where is Melody?", asked Tom.

"Oh, she is in the loo," the sports teacher replied. "Here Tom, no child is allowed a phone! Pass it to me," said the sports teacher.

"WHAT! MY SPOTS TEACHAR DON'T ALLOW ME MY PHONE!!!" shouted Tom.

"No shouting allowed here, boy." said the sports teacher angrily, "AND I DON'T HAVE SPOTS ALL OVER, YOU SEE!"

On Friday, the sports teacher told melody what had happened when he was young, and he told her he wanted a rugby ball.

Melody already knew what he wanted! She had brought a present for the sports teacher, and the gift was a new rugby ball! She had even wrapped it carefully.

Two hours passed, and the other regular students came to the court to play and do sports. The students all changed into their sports uniforms. They went outside the court to do some sports with their lovely teachers. Melody brought the present with her, putting it behind her back, and then spoke to the sports teacher.

"Pardon me, Melody?", asked the teacher excitedly. "Close your eyes or no sports," said Melody seriously.

"Put your hands out," she added.

After six seconds had passed by, she put the present in the teacher's hand and whispered: "Open your sweet, gentle eyes."

"Wow! A present! I don't know why I deserve this! THANK YOU VERY MUCH! ", shouted the teacher. "It's a lovely rugby ball, and it's clean!"

Melody was very happy to see the teacher's surprised and happy expression. She felt that giving this present to her the teacher was entirely the right choice.

Story 4

The Story of the Castle read by Alice

Alice was reading a book about a castle; this is what she read…

A character named Morgan Lewis explored a castle by accident. She also went there by a strange portal but couldn't go back to her home country. The castle from the Middle Ages was tucked away in an ancient forest. Inside the castle, there was a gramophone that played royal music. Some scribes were jotting Latin phrases, to praise God.

The writers were sitting on retro chairs. They were carved out of wood but sometimes gold or silver. They put the brownish paper on a weird-looking table, and then, they jotted them down. Besides, there was the pope, saying he was obliged to God to pray

inside his heart. He seemed to be feeling like floating away from his world.

A portal machinery sound was coming from the castle beside a forest, and there was a lovely girl from a hunter's family, called Maggie, nearby. She was curious about the castle as it had been closed all the time.

One morning, she woke up to hear the strange noise coming from the castle. There was a man in the court!

Then one day. The gate of the castle suddenly opened, and in came a child from the forest. She saw the dim lights and old furniture on Castle Hill. Curiosity had let the child in. There was a long corridor with no end in sight. Suddenly the castle fell silent, and the strange sound died away.

The lights also went out unexpectedly. A boy lit the match in his pocket and walked cautiously forward. She was terrified. Her little heart thudded, but she covered her mouth, took a deep breath, and walked on. Suddenly, an older man appeared a few dozen paces away. The older adult was hideous - his eyes were wide and straight, and he held a strange book in his hand.

The man looked at her and tapped her on the head many times. She looked at the adult because and thought that he looked very kind. The man then spoke.

"Child, come with me!"

She followed the magic. After a long time, the old man handed her a roll of timetable. He told her: "Child, I am the future man of the world. This era is about to be destroyed and the savior is you. I am the time tunnel, and I want to give you this golden cloth as it will be useful in the future. You will be stronger and stronger. Bye! The world is up to you!"

Suddenly, the old man disappeared into the clouds, the castle disappeared, and she had to go home.

Alice felt sleepy, and she already had read two-thirds of the whole book! She decided that she would continue reading this book at school, if she could! She looked at the time, and it was 9:35pm - five minutes past her bedtime, and her parents would be mad at her. Whatever.

Story 5

S abrina's sea adventure!

Sabrina was walking along the beach thinking she hadn't seen Darcy for a long time. It was windy, and Sabrina had her electric-pink wind coat on. It was 6:43p.m., and Sabrina was relaxing in the summer wind.

While she waited, Darcy was in a boat on the river Seine.

Darcy was on the edge of the aisle, and was feeling exhausted! A few minutes later she and Sabrina skittled to the trees on the isle and danced for a while. Sabrina's merfather was in the sea swimming. He swam closer to the girls, and this was when Sabrina got a shock!

"Who are you?! Please don't disturb my friend and me! Get out of my isle! Tell me what your name is," demanded Sabrina, shocked.

Sabrina's face was as red as the devil's horns, but Darcy tried to calm her down.

"Please be calm. I'm sure he's not a thief. He might have come to..." began Darcy, but Sabrina stopped her.

"Came to kill me?" shouted Sabrina.

She then thumped her feet as if the mountains were lighter than her whole body. The ground shook, the entire earth trembled beneath her feet!

"Nope, you are mistaken. I am your merfather! Now, come with me!" demanded Sabrina's merfather.

Under the water, Sabrina couldn't breathe properly. The merfather said that his real name was Marc as Sabrina swam along with him! They arrived in a soggy cave and began to chat.

"Now, my dear. This is called the Transformation Cave, where people transform into beautiful creatures..." began Marc.

Sabrina saw a chair and sat on it. BANG! She was turned into a mermaid! GOOD! Now she can go to the Pearl Castle!

It was five miles away, and luckily, Marc had a SWIMMING BOOST COIN. Marc and Sabrina dived into the sea and began to follow their map's instructions.

GO TO THE CORAL CEREAL, TURN LEFT WHEN YOU CAN SEE THE YELLOW SEAWEED CORRIDOR. LOOK FOR A SIGN THAT SAIS 'TRAPS PROVIDED, THIS WAY'.

NOT TO GET LOST OR HURT, FOLLOW MARC'S LEAD!

Meanwhile, Darcy was tired of waiting, so she fell asleep. Zzzzzzz…

Marc led the way forward to Coral Cereal, before turning left to the yellow seaweed corridor and followed the signs. After a few hours Sabrina was in the Pearl Castle where she greeted the King and Queen. She was needing food and a rest. So, Marc asked the King and Queen if Sabrina could have a dish of food since she was hungry.

After a few days, Sabrina became popular in Rainbow Town, under the sea. Sabrina was happy as a Unicorn.

Darcy had been left alone, and she had gone home by rowing the boat.

The following day Darcy and Sabrina went to the Eiffel Tower and had a wonderful teatime in the restaurant nearby. Sabrina wondered what to do next, then Darcy nudged her and said, "What about shopping? Then can we go to my mother's cake shop and do our icing decorations!"

"Good idea, Darcy! We shall go in a few minutes! Yeah!", replied Sabrina, as she was finishing her chocolate strawberries.

After shopping and visiting Darcy's mother's cake shop near the Eiffel Tower, they went home. But they couldn't fall asleep because of all the excitement!

Story 6

The Magic Wishing tree one

There were three Buttercup children called Matilda, Peter, and Susan. They had a dog named Smarter, and all four of them were all still asleep in their beds... snoring.

It was Friday, June 25th and the bright sun was shining outside. But the snoring children, and their dog, took no notice of the sun or the noisy sound of trucks coming along.

"Good morning, darlings!" Mom shouted excitedly. "We are going to move to a new house, but you'll have to carry your mu mummy's handmade bags."

"Mmm...what? Ice cream?"

"Do you have any cakes here? Yeh! Mrs. Lizzie, are you here?" Peter asked.

"Mrs. Liz, are you here?", he repeated.

"No cakes, Peter, you have overslept! Three, two, one... time to wake up," lsaughed their mum.

Susan Buttercup and Matilda Buttercup were soon eating giant eggs for breakfast. After a while, they called a taxi to go to the train station. After spending 20 minutes on the train, they got off and called another taxi.

They did enjoy that fast train and chattered lost, especially Matilda Buttercup who is a chatterbox! They were chatting for half the time and spent the rest of the time getting ready for the taxi. The driver turned out to be dad! WOW!

At last they arrived at Golden Street, where the houses were as big as a school. When they reached their new home, they made themselves comfortable and then decided to walk towards a nearby forest. Their parents said that they could go, but they must be careful.

On their way they visited a shop that sells magic wishes. Unfortunately, they only had one left. Susan Buttercup said they should buy it and run as fast as possible to the forest.

"Wow! elves and fairies!", shouted Matilda. "Shut up, Matilda, said, Peter.

They decided to climb the grand tree to see who's living there. Climb and climb, they almost reached the top, but Susan was tired.

"Ahh... let's go down because I'm tired," she complained.

"No, you can't. It is too high to jump, and the climb is not easy."

So how do we go down? No idea. Susan began to cry.

Suddenly there was knock on the door behind their back. And the door opened.

"What's that noise? I can't sleep!", groaned a candy-faced man.

"Are you a candy which has a b...", began Matilda, but Peter shushed her.

"You can ride on my slider if you give me some candy," started the candy-faced man, "Do you guys have any?"

It turned out that if the man eats Candy he becomes more handsome.

"No," replied Susan Buttercup.

"For, and my name is Candy Face."

"Wow! Shouted Matilda.

"You can call me Candy," said Candy, "please make me some candies, if you want to slide on my slider, ok?"

19

The children became friends with the man.

L ily's weird speeches!

Lily had a lot of stuff in her head. And she needs to have space of her own in the study room.

She also wanted to a swimming pool. But she wanted the bottom of the swimming pool to be blue, like the color of the sea. Not like a rock pool.

Besides, Lily's daily routine is to do some homework, and everything that happened in her dreams never came true in real life.

That was until the day of her eighteenth birthday, when her mother gave Lily the house of dreams. The house was close to the sea, and there was a marina for yachts... everything was perfect. Now that she had a lovely prominent place to live, all she needed was a seaworthy boat.

Wow! She thought everything was so incredible, just like a dream is happening!

She saw a yacht coming from her little dock, and she jumped on it. Suddenly there was a gust of wind, and it blew her out to sea, as well as her hat into the water. Lily jumped into the water to try and get her pretty hat. Suddenly she felt so cold! There was another wind blowing – it was the air conditioning. She woke up. It was another dream. How disappointing and sad!

Story 8

The potion of snakes

I woke up one morning feeling a little slimy. I looked down at my body and realized I was a snake. I was very scared.

When my mother came in and woke me up, she saw that I was a snake. She was so scared that she turned pale and ran away. I told her it was me, Noreen. But it didn't help. I know that the animal my mother is most afraid of is a snake.

My mother was downstairs making boiled pork and not fried noodles and because she knows snakes don't eat fried noodles.

Although my mother is terrified of snakes, she loves me very much. She is worried that if the snake is me, I will be hungry. So, she makes me my favorite fried eggs and sausage.

When she's done. she quickly changes her clothes and runs out onto the road.

As I began to enjoy my delicious breakfast, everyone outside the house screams because they can see me in our dining room through the window. My mother watched me silently from outside the window, confirming to everyone that I was her dear daughter.

Eventually, my mother overcame her fear and returned to the living room, where she sat on the other side of the sofa and watched me finish my breakfast. I took my last sip of milk, I then slipped into the garden and began to peel. My mother forgot to close the door and saw ten people screaming on the lawn outside our house.

I slipped back in the door and curled up around my mom, smiling with my slimy body, which meant I loved her. We went to the kitchen again to get the ingredients for a potion. I stood up, took the ingredients from the fridge and began to mix them with my tongue.

After drinking some milk, I watch BBC TV news while waiting for the potion to heat up and boil with hot bubbles.

An hour later, the mixture is ready. Not too hot and not too cold, just right. I smell it, but it's too bitter to drink.

I wait for another hour, but nothing had changed. My mother has finally adjusted to my snakelike presence, and she put down a book I didn't finish last night by my side and began to busy herself with housework.

I pour out five milliliters of sugar and begin to mix up the potion again. When I finish, I waited for another hour. It is as if the honey is purely attached to the bee's womb, and it lies there splashing. I drank it in one gulp, and it began to change me. The old snakeskin is gone.

The loathsome snakeskin potion is over.

Story 9

Miranda, the helpful capture

Once upon a time, there was a little girl named Miranda. She was a helpful student, who was humorous and funny, liked to study, and she often helped her mother with the housework. But there was a slight problem at home.

Their house was filled with chocolate because her mother ran a small supermarket next to the pre-prepare school. The store was too small, so her mother kept a lot of goods at home.

But her father was a thief, and he had friends who were also thieves. They were trying to steal the delicious chocolate. Around the whole house and its big garden was an iron fence about three metres high (with spikes on the top), so robbers couldn't jump over or climb over.

On July 23, 1986 (a Tuesday) Miranda caught three robbers who were trying to steal chocolate in the afternoon and she took them to prison.

Miranda had been walking Buster the dog when he smelt someone in the hedge and ran to them. At that time, there were no guns allowed so that no one could shoot from a distance. She followed the robber outside the fence, pulled by Buster, and Miranda called out, "Mama! Buster smelled the robbers!" She caught some of her father's thief friends red-handed, and when she saw them, Miranda was given a prize from her mother. The award was three bars of chocolate.

One of the robbers even made a paper gun, but her dog didn't take the fake weapon seriously. It's totally out of the question to frighten a dog.

Story 10

The Idyllic pizza

There is a chef named John who is known locally for his unique baked pizzas. Chef John never makes any operational mistakes in his work and has always been very confident!

At noon on a sunny Sunday, John is busy at home. Today he wants to try to make a pizza that he has never made before. Today he has invited some of his good friends to his house to taste the new flavor of pizza he is making.

John grabbed some dough and shaped it into various shapes. He was thinking about how to proceed. Just then, his friend Francis arrived. He gave John an idea. He thought John could make the dough into a circle and put an Eiffel Tower on top.

John disagreed with his friend's proposal at first because he didn't have a model of the Eiffel Tower at home. So, Francis volunteered to go to the mall to buy one.

John continued with his work, kneading the dough and humming an Italian song. After a while, the dough was ready. John prepared some green vegetables and pressed them into juice. Francis arrived with his proposed model of the Eiffel Tower.

In addition to the friends John invited, he had two family members coming to taste his new pizza. John's younger sister, who is a young girl with a husky voice, and John's uncle, who has a goatee beard and grey hair, were also invited. The uncle has a chubby beer belly that looks like he could eat an entire pizza.

The expected pizza is finally out of the oven. The circle around the pizza looks like grass, and with a model of the Eiffel Tower, it feels like you're having afternoon tea in the middle of Paris. People were saying this pizza is so good they couldn't bear to eat it and didn't want to cut it.

John's uncle finished his pizza as they were talking! If there were a competition, John should be first.

Story 11

In the middle of the winter

When my young sister and I went out to the forest we didn't know there would be a blizzard.

Icy snowflakes were dancing in the wind. The bone-chilling winter air made my teeth chitter as I walked through the rugged, white blanket of snow. We continued along the wet road when suddenly I heard a loud bang, like a bomb. I was shocked! I've never heard a bomb before. I knew I was scared, and my face turned as white as a blank sheet of paper. It wasn't a bomb, though, it was a very thick branch that had fallen from the tree, just in front of us. If we had walked faster, it would have hit us. The dead  leaves on the branch crunched under our feet as we walked past. I longed to be back in my warm home and sit by the blazing fire.

I was carrying two big bags of my young sister's toys, and she was holding a giant cotton candy that she had just bought at the mall. The cotton candy was soft like pink clouds. The entire marshmallow became crispy as a breadcrumb, and then it turned black because of the cold.

We were cold and hungry, and I thought I saw the steak I liked and would devour like a hawk. Suddenly a gust of cold wind hit me. I called to my young sister, "If you don't want to freeze to death in the snow, throw away your marshmallow and let's run!"

Finally, we ran and slid in the snow like two mice and hurried back home. My uncle, the Principal of St. Marcus's, was in the back garden and couldn't hear us. When he opened the door, he repeated the word 'tea' like a parrot. He said he was waiting for my parents to come back. My father and mother were not at home. My uncle said they had gone to a nearby mall.

As soon as my sister and I walked through the door, icicles fell from us. Looking out at the bad weather and I was glad we're finally home.

Sabrina's sea adventure!

On the beach, the children were playing with balls. Three boys played a UFO game in a small space, and five girls played hide-and-seek. A family of six was swimming, and Mark Owen and Lewis Charters ate ice cream while they walked along the beach.

Five children were swimming in the shallow water near the beach. Their names were Darcy, John, Rema, Sabrina, and Maia. It was indeed a happy day.

"Rema, are mermaids real?", asked Sabrina.

"No, they are not real. You are silly and childish!", replied Rema.

While Sabrina and Rema chatted Darcy, Maya, and John were building sandcastles. Sabrina and Rema had a long chat.

"Reema! Sabrina! Come here! We're leaving the beach!" Sabrina and Rema's parents shouted.

Sabrina and Rema, whose parents are sisters, also live together. But the design of this house is singular. Rema chose the peach, but Sabrina chose the mermaid and the unicorn.

Sabrina's mother, Mathilde, said: "Quiet Reema! Go to the cupboard under the stairs! You're so selfish!" When the speech was over, Rema snorted. She thought, what happened to the peaches? How did Sabrina win?

At the same time as people are turning things into unicorns and mermaids Rema is locked in a cupboard inside the house, and the beach is full of people. Suddenly, a distant siren sounded.

A shark had injured a man. He was a father. Ambulances roared in from all over the place, and they quickly lifted the man away from the hungry shark and took him to the hospital. His blood could still be seen on the sand. His wife and children watched on apprehensively.

Sabrina and her friends were terrified. They come to the beach almost every weekend in the summer, and it's the first time they've seen something like this happen.

The parents didn't want their children to have nightmares and decided to end the beach activities early.

Story 13

Milly's story!

I'm Millie. On the first day of the New Year in 1967, something happened at my school. I studied in the eighth grade - the last year of pre-prepare school. Every day was hectic.

My family had been getting ready for the New Year. Although my classmates are difficult, I tolerate my class, and I believe I will get a good grade.

Why is that, you may ask.

The reason is that I keep a diary, which records what happens, so, I can see my past academic progress.

First, my classmate, who is like a devil, has broken my mother's vases countless times. She came to my house again this week. This time, my mother had just bought a new crystal vase, and she smashed it to pieces, completely irreparable. This made my mother distressed for many days. Especially before the New Year.

As punishment my friend had to help with all the housework.

Deary me! I'm so happy about the sentence she got! She hates doing housework and always makes a mess of the place around her. Everywhere you go, you can see her trail.

Because she broke my mother's favourite vase, her own mother gave her a further punishment!

After what happened, my mom was always worried that my friend would come to my house again. But I told her I don't want to be friends with her again.

Story 14

The story of Anne Frank

I want to share some information from a book I recently read called The Diary of Anne Frank.

Thirteen-year-old Anne moved into the secret annex of her house during World War II. She was born in Frankfurt, Germany. But her parents were Jewish, so she was born a Jew. The Germans bullied the Jews. At that time, the Jews had no state of their own. Not like now, because they have a country called Israel.

While the Germans were doing their unkind things, the Russian army helped the Jews and won. It's a pity that all the Frank family are dead except Otto.

Otto. H. Frank, the father of Anne Frank, died in 1980. He found Anne's diary and published it. It caused a sensation because it documented the actual persecution of Jews by the Germans at the time.

It's part a sad story, and part not so terrible.

Hi, Anne's boyfriend is knocking at the door. Anne's mother and Mr. Van Dahn went out to say hello. Anne's family is living in a secret annex.

Her family also went to the secret annex and wore multiple layers. They look like they're going to the freezer, but they do this so that they can bring more clothes.

They went to the annex building and had a worrying week.

Only read on if you are okay with being upset.

What did the Franks fail to do? It said Annie wanted to go to the gym, but she wasn't allowed, and the gym was closed.

Annie's father, Otto, is about to go to his office, and he's allowed because it's under the warehouse.

Edith, Anne's mother, wanted to go

to the salon, but she couldn't, as it's against the regulations. Even poor Margot can't play table tennis with her friends!

Because of the law and regulations, Annie's cat, Tommy, Bouche, must stay behind. Anne was miserable because she loved Peter, who lived with her in the warehouse.

Peter also has a grey cat, but it's too noisy. At one point, the cat almost led the Germans to discoverer the family.

Anne wanted to take her cat, whose name was Moortjie, but he might not be quiet, so her parents decided not to allow it. Anne was afraid that Peter would marry someone else.

For Peter, the punishment of not seeing Anne was terrible. He didn't even have a chance to be a good man to her.

Anne wanted to make sure that Peter's little room became more comfortable. She wanted Peter to be happy and comfortable, not a hardwood bed without a quilt.

Anne also wanted Peter to be as happy as possible.

She suggested that he put a cushion and a bookshelf beside the table for the Franks. But the most important thing was to follow the rules and not see friends. So, they had to hide and had keep quiet to avoid being spotted by the Germans.

Unfortunately, Anne and Margot were found dead in the camp. They were buried somewhere nearby.

Anne wrote a diary entry to prove that it was hard to hide. But   unfortunately, she had to do it for safety reasons.

Anne's father, Otto, published her diary to let people know how difficult it was to hide during the war. War is also very terrible.

The book made me change my view of Germans. I'm so sad.

39

A tale of Roald Dahl's childhood

If you have read the book *'Charlie and the Chocolate Factory'*, you must know Roald Dahl.

In the last term of form one, because the school was closed, the English teacher asked us to learn this book online. My mom bought a set of the author's books. It was then that I got to know Roald Dahl and began to read his books.

The following story was told to me by one of my online lesson teachers. His name is Francis.

Roald Dahl as a child in Norway was with his mother and they were going to the doctor's house. Although she had said that Roald had some adenoids, he still wasn't sure what it meant.

So that day, little Dahl went to the doctor's house to find out. He sat on a chair, and the doctor had a mirror strapped to a band. The doctor was having a whispered conversation with Roald's mother about what would happen to dear little Dahl.

Little Dahl was sitting on the doctor's chair, then a nurse came in holding an apron and an enamel bowl. The doctor boiled a pot and dipped a metallic stick in the water. It was sharp at the end and regular at the other.

So far so terrific. The doctor told the nurse to make little Dahl wear the red apron and hold the bowl.

When the operation was over, the Dahl family went home, and granny told little Dahl to sit down and rest. The chair he sat on was moved right next to his grandma.

Four stories

1. Wendy was cursed

Once, a little girl named Wanda was in her house. She loved to make up stories and read them to her little sister. Her little sister was always asking for just one more, I promise! If you wonder what her little sister's name is, it is Wendy Bake.

Now, Wendy is a reticent girl. She has many friends, just because she doesn't disturb other people's reading time.

Wanda's story made her little sister laugh! This is when things start to go strange.

Wendy usually comes home with a cap on, but today, she wore a scarf. She doesn't carry her own bag but had her friend's shopping bag.

Wanda asked, "Why did you carry that bag?"

Wendy didn't reply, and she was deadly silent.

They went indoors, and they became chattier and chattier.

Wanda suddenly noticed a green spot on her sister's forehead when she took her hat off. She shouted, "Cursed child! Cursed child!"

2. Sweet lemon isn't real

Once in the town of Dudley, a family decided to have some lemonade.

There was Sam, the father, Julie, the mum and Brandon Sky, the child. Mum made some cakes, and dad made the lemonade. Unfortunately, dad mistook sugar for salt and poured it into the lemonade.

At resting time, everybody took a cup of lemonade and started drinking:

"Dad, why is the lemonade so sweet? Please add more salt", said the child.

Dad added more salt, he but made a mistake again! Sky pointed, "Look, mum! Dad is so mistakable!"

Mum sighed - she was thinking the same. She thought Sweet lemonade isn't natural.

3. Why you are... SO HANDSOME!

Mr. Molly wasn't loved by his students, but he was adored by the headmistress.

People from all around the world went to that school, to see him! WHOA! But Miss Sophie, the headmistress, got him first. He chose her to be his wife.

One day, he married Miss Sophie. They went on to have two children.

Marcus, Mr. Molly's brother, became an uncle. And Helix, Miss Sophie's little sister, became an aunty.

They lived contentedly ever after.

If you wonder where the Molly family are, they are in a particle of this page!

4. The Fashionable Fairy

Amaretto was a fairy who was very fashionable. If you see inside her closet you'll see sections of clothing, hair accessories, sunglasses, shoes (although she sometimes goes bare foot!), handbags, hats, a few earrings, coats, skirts, tops, dresses, and four pairs of high heels.

Amaretto woke up in the flower, which is where she lives. She got a leaf and squeezed some petal powder on it, then found some water in the garden.

Finally she brushed her teeth by making the leaf as a tunnel then pouring the powder through it. The way she washed her face is straightforward, and everyone knows that except babies and toddlers. She was now ready for the party, and dressing time! Yee-Pee!

She covered her naked body with some leaves and then used her magic wand to make her wings disappear. She then took out a petal sewed-together dress, which has teeny tiny patterns on it. So far so good. She then put on the dress and her leaf-made simple sandals, and she loved her outfit so much!

M y diary

The diary of a young girl...

September 13, 1956.

I started my day at this new school. My name is Lillian. J. Everything is so exciting and intense.

September 15, 1956.

Honey, I should give you a name. Teresa. At school, I have no time to write to you. I will try to spare more time to be with you.

September 16, 1956.

Dear Teresa, I finally have time! Well, who's that? Don't be so arrogant. I'm going to bed. Good night! Sleep well!

September 18, 1956.

Today was supposed to be the game day, but because Tilly got dirty and then got hurt, the game couldn't go on as scheduled. I think she fell at 14:34. Maybe I shouldn't have joked about "breaking your leg" the other day.

September 20, 1956.

Dear Teresa, Tilly's wound is nasty. But if you are my mother, please give me something that can cure her! She was my teammate and friend. She is so fond of sports. It is such a frustrating thing that she can't participate in the competition.

September 24, 1956.

Honey, Miss Keble told me not to cut corners. But she did it herself! Oh, here she comes. I don't have time to write any more. Goodbye!

December 15, 1956.

Honey, because it's the Christmas party coming up, I went to bed early at six o 'clock! Not my senior head nurse! I must hide you, my sweet Barbie. Good night!

Best of all, they were edited by Noreen S.

Holiday at the beach

This is a story about two sets of twins who go on holiday – away from their charming secret garden.

Mary and Maria are twins. So are Janet and Jane. Both sets of twins live in the same building. They call it the Green Building. What's more, it has a secret garden. What do you think they'll find in this private garden?

Things like tulips, like huckleberries, like buttercups, perhaps. There is a bell, and there are sunflowers, roses, and many other beautiful flowers.

There is more than flowers in the secret garden. There's a tree, a hedge, leaves, even white stones and marble fountains.

Because the twins' parents are so wealthy that they can buy a luxury holiday ticket. If you're wondering, this is just an introduction. It's time for the twins to go to bed. Good night!

Jane and Maria are staying at home, so Janet and Mary are going out. Mary is wearing a cornflower dress. Janet and Mary are best friends, how lucky!

They waited in the car for Dad with her mother, who looked beautiful. Dad locked up the house then checked the windows, the front door, the glass shed, and the garage door.

They're ready to go!

They go! Zoom! Zoom!

They go to Bronchitis Beach to relax, and enjoy some swimming, sunbathing, surfing, and windsurfing.

They spent four days at the beach, staying in the beach house they built.

But one day, an adventure began.

"Mal, get me the soy sauce, please! Thank you!", requested Janet, who was eating a strange breakfast.

"Miss Janet, there's no salt, only soy sauce!", Mal shouted, which made Janet very angry.

"I said soy sauce, not salt! Will you come and get me that?", cried Janet angrily.

"Janet, oh, please calm down. You've knocked the whole house down - people will see us going to the toilet, and no one will like that, will they?" Mary interrupted.

There were ice cream trucks on the beach and children enjoying the waves. Next to the beach were massage centres and toy stores.

A woman in her forties or fifties approached them and asked if anyone wanted a massage at a massage centre. Because everyone said yes, the lady was delighted. She smiled. She knew that these two families of eight would bring her a good income. Both mums chose full-body massages and facials.

Both sets of twins copied their mums as they are obsessed with beauty.

The two dads chose Thai massages and foot massages, because their legs were tired. The excellent day passed.

Story 19

The rumours

Someone at the school said that David's sister's friend had told him that Mary Mayne was disturbing the Waynes who lived next door.

Although they were neighbours, the Waynes had never met the Maynes. The Waynes hadn't been out much since they moved in.

Not many of the neighbours had seen them — they were a very mysterious couple.

It is also worth mentioning that Madame Lilongwe and Father Mace, who did not always see eye to eye, finally got married and got on very well. But many disagreed, saying they were often noisy and often unfollowed on Instagram.

It turns out that where there are people there are always rumours.

Story 20

The horrible holiday houses

Martina Lawsone's great grandfather owned the Horrible House.

Martina liked art and she also liked exploring too. Her mother wanted her to become a scientist if she kept digging, but an artist if she continued to like art.

Martina had a friend called Nokia Nottingham. Nokia was the granddaughter of an artist, and she had a boyfriend who wanted to be a scientist. So, they call themselves the Triple Three.

Other students created the phrase 'Triple Three' with names like Soviet or Sonia, who are twins. Some people call Soviet 'MAD' SALT GIRL or called Sonia' SUGAR KINDNESS SWEETNESS'.

Daphne Downer was Martina's fan but she couldn't join in because of her smallpox - she had gone spotty and had scars after they faded.

"Hey, Martina! Want an idea for a fantastic exploring place?", asked Nokia's boyfriend, who was named Cecil Henderson.

"Really? Yes please, but don't let Mary hear it," replied Martina.

So, one day, they explored Martina's grandfather's house that used to be a hospital. They started at the entrance.

They went to the bathroom, where Cecil fainted. They then saw a bar full of broken wine glasses. They went to a cupboard and saw a rusted metal box with the label 'CAUTION!'

The metallic box was bolted and locked, but they found a key beside it. They saw the hidden lock and put the key into it - click! - it opened and out came another box. This smaller package was labeled 'PRECIOUS!'

The key was on the top of the box, and the Triple Three found precious jewels.

The twins found another box, which also contained a great surprise – beneath all the cobwebs was more jewels.

Story 21

A n awkward time

In the Andreas a girl has won an award at her school. But it must be received in a dress.

It was supposed to be a happy day, but the problem was that she didn't like skirts or dresses. So, she had to endure her father's cruelty and was forced to wear a skirt.

When she arrived at school, no one had ever seen her in a skirt before. All her boyfriends and girlfriends called her rude names and laughed at her. She wanted to cry, but that would show she was weak, so she kept silent. She pretended not to care about everything. Deep down, she wanted to turn into a mouse and hide under the floor.

When she had her first lesson, her teacher Miss Jane said, "Every cloud has a silver lining. You look beautiful!"

The girl said, "Thank you, but I prefer trousers to skirts and dresses!"

Finally, she accepted what she looked like in a dress. She thought it was beautiful to wear a skirt, though not as convenient as trousers.

Story 22

Go to the dentist

I am Keira. So far, I've hurt a leg while skateboarding and I, unfortunately, also lost half of my teeth. My wisdom tooth is healing well, but I must have it removed as it always makes me feel very uncomfortable.

It's my first time to see the dentist. Deep inside, I feel nervous. It wasn't as bad as I thought! There were signs on the walls inside the clinic where I had to wait. I didn't expect so many people at the dentist's.

When I entered, the room was spotless and white. When the nurse motioned to sit on the chair that looked like a bed, I cried.

I felt so scared and helpless.

Finally, the doctor gave me an anaesthetic. With a few simple manoeuvring skills, he pulled my tooth out in a matter of minutes. I felt no pain at the time. I was just worried that it would hurt when I go to bed and I can't sleep. It's what it feels like to go to the dentist. It's not that scary.

Story 23

Characters' introduction

Fiona was an eight-year-old girl and had brown hair and green eyes. Uranus was her boyfriend who was the same age and looked like her.

Charlotte was a ten-year-old girl who was always frantic; when her rubber went missing, she would yell and yell at the people beside her. She only had two friends like Madeleine.

Madeleine was probably the politest member of the Hide and Seek group. She had blonde hair and blue eyes.

Victoria was not the politest - more in the middle. She always acted very royally indeed, but I don't mean that she is related to any queen or king. Victoria wanted to be a good actress, but she could not choose what part she wanted to act. She still looked like Fiona the same colour of eyes and the same blonde hair.

Relationships

Fiona and her boyfriend Uranus were the furthest apart in their family tree. Madeleine and Victoria were cousins, and of course, close friends! Charlotte was related to Uranus.

One Saturday night

One Saturday night, Fiona, Uranus, Charlotte, Madeleine, and Victoria all went to the St. Maria's School for Girls.

Victoria suggested that they play hide and seek while everyone was sleeping so they wouldn't be so bored! Uranus wasn't very good at hide and seek because he always jumped over the fence or shouted until he calmed down. It was 11:30 in Elmwood Street and people still slept in their beds.

"I'll count to ten - nine, eight, seven, six, five, four, three, two... one! Here I come!", counted Victoria, "Get ready!"

"Ugh, I'll never win!", muttered Madeleine as she hid in the cleaning cupboard.

Charlotte was going to hide beside Madeleine, but Madeleine budged her out. Charlotte got cross and shouted: "DON'T EVEN BUDGE ME OFF! URANUS IS BETTER THAN YOU!"

"You'd better run, or I'll tell Victoria where to catch you," replied Madeline.

"Anyway, all Uranus does is get mad and stamp on my foot!" she whispered.

Fiona hid in the dusty cupboard then put some mops in front of her as well as a cleaning brush on the top. She also had written CLEANING CUPBOARD on the door with the words HAZARD OF CHOKING ON FUMES AND DUST beneath.

The Ending

At last Victoria found Charlotte because the cabinet door was left open. Madeleine and Fiona won the game, and both got a bar of silver and a pink bookmark from Victoria. They had a perfect time before their parents woke up.

"What's all that noise? We shall go and see," they enquired.

Then the children were in great trouble.

Maria and Marie

"Who threw this muddy ball into my garden?" asked Miss Smith - Marie's vicious neighbour.

Maria and Marie were sisters. They both have green eyes, but they don't have the same hair colour. One has yellowish-brown with strands of dyed pink. She also wears a bow on her head when it is Easter, and a Christmas hat when it is the Christmas holidays. The other sister was much older and has black hair. She has the nickname 'permanent worker one'  given to her by their neighbour, Miss Smith. The older sister was always rude to Miss Smith.

"Who stole my watch?" asked Miss Smith.

"Not me! It's Maria, she did it!" said Marie.

"N-N-NOT ME!" she stammered in response.

"Come here now, follow me", said Miss Smith.

But suddenly Miss Smith felt a cavity in her mouth, as she had never appropriately brushed her teeth. Maria was kind enough to take Miss Smith to the dentist. They lined up in the queue, but Miss Smith shouted, "GO away! I shouldn't be at the back!".

Then she grew even more impatient.

Finally, it was her turn to be seen. She saw sharp tools and white walls when she entered as well as models of the mouth, a first aid box and bag, and a cabinet. She grew scared of what she saw. She turned to run but was held by the nurse, who said, "Sit down, for if you run, I will open your mouth for you."

So, she sat down and did what she was told. She tried to yell when the dentist said he was doing an operation. "What's your name?", asked the dentist.

"Miss Back - you make me angry, sir," she growled. He started to run away but came back and spoke once more.

"It's very mean of you to say that, miss. But what's your real name?".

"Just that, you ignorant person!" she replied again.

"You are Mr. Huh, instead of Dr. Happy!" said Miss Smith, looking annoyed.

An hour later the operation was over.

When Maria laughed, Miss Smith figured that it was Marie who stole her watch.

Story 25

The Ancient Scroll

Contents:

Chapter 1

I am Carlo. I work for secretary, Terry in office 246. My mother's name is Clara, and she's thirty-five. My father's name is Charles. He is thirty-eight years old. My mother's birthday is on August 24, and my father's birthday is on July 31.

I forgot to tell you that I have a sister of the same age as me and the same birthday month - the day was only three days more. Guess what? It was March 24, the day of my mother's birthday, only another month.

So, my name's called Carlo. Because my sister and I are both named Carla we often get mixed up. But I am a boy and she is a girl.

Our names both begin with 'Carl.' My sister's end vowel is an 'a', and mine is an 'o'.

Understand now? It usually happens to boys but not girls. Why not girls? Because girls are generally polite, so they don't care about our vowels which is good.

This is all, and my uncle died five years ago.

I hope that you can guess my birthday.

Chapter 2

So, you know me from my introduction. It's not over yet!

I have a friend called Max, and he has a secret gang which solves problems. They are called 'The Detectives.'

Max is so intelligent and quick – and he has a gang of eight people.

They are Martha, John, Max, Ryan, Carlo, Oscar, Melody and Barker.

Do you know what Barker is? Well, guess what barks! Yes, dogs bark! Barker is a name for a dog.

I live at Newspaper Cottage on Barn Street. SU78 2WE.

You probably know why it's called newspaper cottage.

No it's not made of newspaper. But it's all about my dad. He's a funny guy, who loves reading the newspaper.

But we're off track! Whenever something weird happens to me, Max solves the problems.

You see, this is all I can say. Maybe it's because Max doesn't allow me to say too much.

Goodbye!

Chapter 3

Living next to my house, is a girl named Madeleine who has a little sister called Melody.

Now, Melody is from angry stock, and she never listens to anybody at all - not even her parents!

So, the day began well, and Madeleine just finished her practice exam-paper. She clicked open her laptop and watched the footage from her covert security camera.

She saw a thief putting a colorful, strange object into a pinkish-colored cream, and then she messaged John to go to the ice-cream cart.

"John! Buy a block of ice, then look out for the machine in the pink cream on the cart!"

So, John went to the cart and spotted it but couldn't pull it out. Even more thrilling, the shopkeeper spotted him trying to pull it out.

At last, the shopkeeper helped him and then John used the phone to call the police.

The thief cried bitterly and was sent to jail.

A nne and Peter's secret

Anne was a kind, secretive person. However, she was also a sensitive girl as well as being imaginative and kind-hearted.

She never makes anyone angry, but her boyfriend doesn't know that Anne wants to marry Peter.

Anne tries to make everyone happy all the time, but things aren't always perfect. Some of them are not her cup of tea. But, of course, she still makes her boyfriend happy without letting him in on the secret.

Peter liked Anne too, but he didn't know she liked him. He always assumed that Anne wanted other people. And Anne thought he liked someone else.

So, one day, he couldn't wait to tell Anne, "I love Anne, not Ursula."

That's great! Anne likes Peter, too. Peter waves to her. Perfect couple.

Ursula didn't know that Anne liked Peter.

Story 27

The pink sofa

"Mrs. Win, can I go out and get some pizza toppings?", asked Hannah the cook, who didn't have the ingredients to make some pizza.

Hannah worked in Mrs. Win's house. She was new to the family. Mrs. Win's husband had died and was not well off.

Today she's getting ready for the big weekend party. She used to work for a billionaire, but her boss fired her for overeating. Hannah thought it was a good idea to give hungry children some peace and happiness.

"Mrs. Win, I have some money to buy vegetables. But I will try to save some money to buy toys."

And away she went, the lousy shopping bag swinging fast in the cold, damp air.

The walk was quickly over, and she soon came to the food section, then the toy section.

She bought a racing car and a motorcycle for the boy, and then a doll and a Sylvanian family to suit the girl.

She took a long look at the couch she liked in the home area. She wanted very much to give a couch to Mrs. Win because she saw that the couch in her house was so old that it creaked when she sat on it. But she didn't have any money left. You should have seen the look on the children's faces when the cook came home, and their faces were so full of delight.

And Granite spends most of her time chopping off the doll's head while the mother doesn't seem to notice.

Granite giggled and thought, "Ha! You're a fat little boy! I want to chop - chop-chop!"

The cook then shouted, "Granite! You go back to your bedroom and don't chop off this delicate doll's head! Or I'll cut yours off and you'll be in pain!"

Granite then cried.

"Miss Hannah! Don't yell at my beautiful daughter, and she won't chop off the doll's house or their heads!"

"Your salary is going down," she yelled.

"I used to work for a billionaire," said Hannah, "and I got fired, and by the way, I'm going to show you the victim's room!"

After seeing the room Mrs. Win fainted and said, "You are right, but don't hurt her. I'm going to tell her to stay outside…"

A month later.

A flying piece of furniture flew toward Mrs. Win's house and landed in front of her door.

"For Mrs. Win" was written on a sign, along with her phone number and home address.

She was stunned. She said to Hannah, "I have found something that can fly in the air! Could you give me some volunteers? I need someone to help me move in! "

The neighbors all pitched in to help move the sofa. "What a beautiful couch! And pink, which Mrs. Win likes!" they said. "Who gave it to you?"

"This couch can fly!? It's amazing!"

"I don't know, and it's none of your business!" said Hannah.

"Well! Oh, my gosh! Rude!"

The neighbors were not pleased with the way she spoke.

Then everyone was gone, and Hannah was at peace! She smirked and said: "Oh, it's really magical, and it is the couch that I have a crush on."

Then she smiled.

Story 28

Maisie and Laura's little caravan

Part I: intro to characters

Cousins Maisie was 10 years old, and Laura was exactly one year younger as they had the same birthday.

Laura, who has ginger hair and green eyes, was shorter than Maisie, who had curly brown hair and sea blue eyes.

Part II: Chatting

"Can you see that, Maisie? That looks like a merry-go-round! Can we play there?", asked Laura, looking excited.

"Course not without parent's permission! Well, that's not a merry-go-round! It's a coloured wheel with choices, and it's not a circus either!", replied Maisie.

Maisie was wondering if any burglars were peeking at them without-out them noticing.

"Huh, you always think of burglars! Can you change your mind a bit, otherwise I will go on a caravan trip without you," said Laura. "For you must get away from your strange thoughts if you want to be friends with me!"

"LAURA! YOU MAKE MY MIND EXPLODE!," roared Maisie.

"PLEASE KEEP QUIET", she continued.

Maisie's parents call her 'Chilly' because her temperature goes up when she's in a temper.

Part III: After the fight

"Maisie, daisy, you are so gay."

"Oh you have a temper and you are my chilly."

"Hey oh you're red, just because you're shy," so sang Laura.

"Laura is rude to me!" replied Maisie, who was getting in a temper again.

(Half an hour later)

"QUIET MAISIE, SIT DOWN AT THE OFFICE AND LAURA, YOU GO TO BUY ICE CREAM FOR YOURSELVES!" shouted mum. "LAURA, GO AND LEAVE THIS ROOM! USE YOUR POCKET MONEY!", she continued, as Laura left the room.

"NOW, MAISIE. I AM VERY, VERY, VERY, VERY, VERY DISAPPOINTED IN YOU," mum looked disappointed.

"YOU SHOULD BE DOING YOUR HOMEWORK."

(A day afterward)

Part IV: Caravan renting

"Guys! I have rented Mr. Leary's caravan, for it can camouflage perfectly with the flowers! Who wants to come?" asked Laura, who was celebrating her birthday.

"Zack, Layla, Moi, Geranium, Hugo and Kay will come! Mum will show the ones who stay behind how to do the maze!" she added.

"Ugh, the mud again!" moaned Maisie.

"Dad, take Maisie to the grounds! Don't let her go and send her to the stairs in the garden that leads to the lasers!" instructed Laura, whose parents were scientists.

Zack, Layla, Moi, Geranium, Hugo and Kay went on the caravan trip. It was the girl's job to do the weaving and for the rest to do the cooking.

Story 29

Mia, the plumber

The story may not be accurate, and it is perhaps false.

The girl is a plumber's assistant, and this is her diary. The text is typed in light green. Some people stress that.

Diary Title: Day: January 19, 2003.

Diary:

My dear, I can't believe my eyes.

I want to be a part-time plumber – or I want to be an assistant plumber.

Just because I'm a girl doesn't mean I can't do a man's job. Did you hear that?

Does anyone think I'm weird?

Maybe it's because I always think I'm so sensitive.

Now, I'm tired. I want a cocktail of juice. I like the taste.

Story 30

Egypt explored

CONTENTS:

Chapter 1

A wave in

The waves are shining beautifully today. My sister and I were swimming along, near the beach, quite merrily. I also have a brother, but he was upset right now.

By the way, the waves are coming in! We tried to swim back to shore, but the current in the water had gripped us tight!

We couldn't do backwards or come forwards!

If you want to know why my brother was upset, he misses his video games.

My sister is six years younger than me, and my brother is 15 years older than me.

A wave splashes over us both! We are soaked from head to toe.

I finally got out of the sea, then asked for ice cream.

Chapter 2

The relaxing beach

"MERCI AU AVOIR!", said Sir Kevin, leaving a trail of petals.

On the beach, it was very relaxing. Some people were drinking cocoa, and some had coconut shells to play with. People lay on benches, and others were swimming. All the children seemed to be playing happily, and they were trying their very best to pile up the shimmering sand to create sandcastles - some were small, and some were huge – all of them spread over the sand.

Two people were doing something odd. A mother and father were being cruel to each other and making a mess. The mum shouted at us to follow the heaps of sand she was leaving.

We were heading towards the west, when we saw a girl dropping her ice cream because her brother Tom had pushed her. It's Polly Pocket.

81

Chapter 3

Why don't you stop

I was in a firing range, blowing the cover down.

Tommy was ruining everything. He ate every dessert by sneaking them to the shell table when we weren't looking.

My hair was blowing in every direction.

If you wonder what me and my little sister's names are, she is Madeline, and I'm called Jessica!

Tommy is stealing all our fun.

Well, it's late. We're going home.

Chapter 4

Sometimes, it's late!

We're running to mummy and daddy in their car. They looked at each other and nodded. We didn't know why—oh, my head's burning. I can feel it.

I think that we are going to Egypt, to explore.

But I don't think it was a sensible idea.

We drove home, and we read in my parent's car.

We're stuck. We can't escape the heat on a sunny day like this. We need more water than usual.

I'm over talking about this.

We arrived home, and we need to pack.

I'm out of breath!

Chapter 5

Dad decides that we need something

"For the family, I will announce all the items we'll need, dad explains.

"Towel, three jugs of clear water, thin clothes, the special mode to build a house, a tv, three boxes, two caps, dresses for girls and shorts for boys - don't forget the shirts as well, Ricky & Martin!"

"A sewing machine will not be allowed on a plane, so that we will use a private one, ha!" he added.

(An hour later)

"Everything I said is now packed? Good. Now off we go!"

Dad went to the car, and everyone huffed as they drove around Park Lane Street.

(Forty minutes of rough driving later)

"Okay. Really? Hmm... top price and we need it so. No extra payments... umm. I don't think that is... Huh, why! Now, bye chancellor!"

Dad ended the meeting, and then he went to type another code in for another session.

"Hi! This is Rufus Daniel…"

"Oh, Mark? You? Okay. So, try to get a price for a plane to Egypt. Here, this is the £100,000,000 I am going to give you.

"Buy me a plane now, please, thanks! I will throw up a nice party if you get me a good deal. Bye."

(30 minutes later)

"OK. Get in, guys! Are we ready? Let's go!"

Chapter 6

My sister was yelping like a dog!

The driver was flying the plane. Good.

"Miaow! I can't wait!"

"OK. Heroize. Stop. Your nonsense! You're grounded now!" shouted mum. She does that a lot!

"Hmm…Ice lolly, please. A box of them at the… OK. Thanks. Bye!"

Chapter 7

Bother! He does that every time!

"Sammy? Can you stop dancing?" requested Heroize.

"No," replied Sammy.

"WHY? You're so mean! Argh!" shouted Heroize again.

Mum and dad barged in and then shouted that the children were grounded in their bedrooms. They both quarreled again for some time.

"Do you like pie?" asked Sammy.

"No."

"Yes?"

Cause no, and I didn't say "YES."

"But now you did."

"OK, I am not trying to be mean, but you are just keeping saying yes and me no. So go to your room and not my bedroom, and then we'll be ungrounded soon enough."

"OK, miss moody, moody…"

"SHHhhh," shushed mum and dad.

"You're not allowed to talk either."

"Mum, I just told Sammy to go to his bedroom."

"That doesn't count, so you have another chance."

"You'd better shush."

"Mm... why!" Heroize quickly replied but then mum and dad closed their bedroom door.

The windfall

I usually go out for a walk with my parents after dinner. As usual, my dad noticed it was sunny so, after our dinner, and suggested we would go to the supermarket.

But suddenly I couldn't see them. I was lost. I fell into a hole, and it was pitch-black.

An hour later, I was in a spaceship and floating in space! I met an alien whom I always wanted to talk to - but I still wanted to call my parents.

The alien's name is **AITE TYI**, and he says his two fingers can turn into an actual phone! I'll try, but all the other aliens have come to listen to my language!

I was eager to try it, although worried it wouldn't work - but it did.

My mom asked me where I was? I told them I had accidentally fallen into a hole.

My dad was speechless because I had called him, too.

I was worried that I would never get back up to see them or something magical would happen.

AITE TYI took me by the hand and said he would show me a base in outer space.

First, he took me to the hall where all the aliens were! Then he took me to a swimming pool full of water.

Then, he took me to the science lab, where aliens were researching medicine.

They were also producing some **CORONAVIRUS** drugs. It surprised me because recently, I have been trying to mix various potions with the scientific knowledge I learned in school to create a specific medicine.

The world had been thrown into disarray by the virus and was in desperate need of this drug. So, I asked the aliens to give me some specific drugs and formulas to treat the coronavirus and save the planet.

AITE TYI said he had it ready for me and would put it in my pocket later.

He walked up to the enormous oval table and asked me if I wanted to sleep, so I stayed there for the night.

A pink halo surrounded it. I had a hard time falling asleep.

Once asleep I don't know how long it took for me to wake up.

AITE TYI took me to the garage, and I automatically rose to the door of the flying saucer.

He landed the flying saucer in my garden. I showed my parents the coronavirus drugs and recipe I had in my pocket.

They were excited to see their precious daughter back. I was excited to use the drugs and the formulas that I didn't invent.

The First term at Amber Towers

Tina was still in her house adoring her new glowing uniform and her skirts. She loved them so much.

Her mummy was calling her.

"Are you ready to ride the fast train to Amber Towers?"

"Please be ready by two o'clock in the afternoon!"

Tina's mummy's voice echoed around the whole house.

"Hmm... nothing better than my new glowing uniform."

"Everybody will love me more than Gina Dickens - she's the worst of my old classmates!" thought Tina.

"Get ready. Run to our taxi before it changes its mind!" shouted mummy, even louder than before.

Tina's dad was the taxi driver, and he drives her whenever she goes out.

Finally, they all arrived at the train station on time, and the train porter said it would leave in ten minutes.

When she arrived at school, she was super excited.

When a blonde-haired girl named Britney said that there would be a disco party in the hall in 10 minutes, she became even more excited. It's a school tradition on the first day of a new term.

On her way to her accommodation, she passed the school farm garden. When she saw cabbages and carrots, which she liked, she asked her teacher for if she could have some seeds to plant at home.

Then she went back to the school hall to party. The first day of school was so much fun!

Story 33

The Famous Fifteen

The Bella was doing her homework on a bench, next to the road.

"Brr! I'm cold! What happened to the sun today? It just looks warm and hot," wondered Bella.

"Sometimes the sun does look warm and hot, but it isn't warm or hot! Poor Ice Cream! Just see the weather icon, darling!" said Bella's mum.

Sally came by and said, "Hello! Want to dance at my house? No one wants to?".

"Mum...yes?" asked Bella.

"I'll come this evening, where the sun never has a chance!"

Sally then hurried up the road to go home.

A few hours later Bella knocked at Sally's door. "Thanks for coming Bella! You're so kind! Follow me!"

Knock! Knock! Knock! Knock!

"Hide," whispered Sally.

A woman in pink and four men in black came in, when Sally answered the door, they then banged the door shut.

The woman grabbed Sally then left the room. "Getaway NOW!" she roared. "Bring your friend wherever she is, then run away to Turtle Shallow Island NOW."

"Take the opportunity to share the secret with all your friends in your neighbourhood," she continued.

"The Men will otherwise grab you and kidnap you. So go on, NO harm will be waiting FOR YOU."

"Argh!" cried Sally as fake as she could.

They all went to Turtle Island, where it is safe.

Story 34

The Secret Nine Society

Once upon a time, there were two children named Harry and Harissa.

Harry was ten years old, and Harissa was nine.

They were walking with their other girlfriend, Lily, and talking about how to make pizza.

Lily said, "Can we make pizza with lots of cheese?"

Harris responded, "No. pizza is too ordinary. I want to make a cake like that for all the children. We can set up a secret organisation to do this."

"I'm the boss! Code is root and sand," he added.

The members of the organisation became Lily, Emma, Pam, Sam, Sandy, Kate, and Leo.

Their snacks included cakes, cupcakes, jellies, Mississippi soft cakes, and of course, each member had a piece.

Lily said, "Oh! I love it! It tastes better than any other cake out there."

Nine days later, Harry and Harissa wrote a letter to seven other friends…

I'm going to open our dream cake factory in the woods. Please come to the bright forest at nine o'clock tomorrow morning and wait for the trumpet to play.

If you hear a trumpet, there will be a red flag in the tree to the right, and somewhere close by there's a spiral staircase. Climb up the stairs until you see a blue mat. Got it?

The seven friends set off for the forest, with Lily driving the big truck. Finally, they arrived at the forest, everyone found the stairs and then saw a blue cushion. When they finally arrived at the destination, they visited the cake making factory.

The cake factory was breath taking!

After sourcing all the ingredients, they worked together to make 100 different cakes. Everyone in the whole forest could smell the cake.

Then the partners worked together to carry the cake to the shop at the front of the forest park.

Customers were waiting patiently at the viewing platform. The customers were amazed when they finally got the cake.

Story 35

The ghost of soups

Once upon a time, there was a poor barber whose wife was always angry about the lack of food in their house.

She always moaned, "Bad hairdresser! Why did you marry me? "

"You should burn as your punishment!"

She would spank him on the buttocks and back with a broom until he was black and blue.

One day, the poor barber decided to go to a village to earn his living and not return until he became rich. On his way he passed the edge of the ghost forest and lay down next to a scary-looking banana tree. A ghost appeared.

"Who are you?" the ghost asked. "You are an enemy!" it continued, "get out of the beauty zone where I sleep! Did you hear what I said? Get out!"

Despite being afraid the barber stood up bravely. As he turned to run away the ghost stopped him.

"I'll eat you!" it warned. "Show me your bag, and I'll let you go."

The barber decided to open his bag. But before unclasping the top, he said: "Well, my bag is full of ghosts, and I have decided to make a ghost soup.

"I will catch you before you can eat me."

The ghost disappeared. The sun came out, and the barber became a very famous. He also became a rich man in the village. His vicious wife dared not bully him anymore.

The Spirit of Midnight

There was a low-income family in the north. They were so poor that they could not afford a piece of bread or fish and chips.

The Spirit of Midnight.

One day, the husband was laying a new carpet. That night he heard footsteps and did not know who they belonged to. When he looked out of the open window he saw it was an elf!

The elf looked up and said, "Our master is the princess of the Shining Land, and she said she needed to wear a blue dress. We saw your beautiful cloth. Will you make one for our master?"

As the elf spoke, a further 11 elves emerged from the shadows.

The husband was unsure what to do.

"We saw you making a dress for your daughter's doll," continued the first elf.

"All right," the husband said.

"Good, if you make us that dress, we'll give you anything to make you rich," the elf promised.

An hour passed, then two hours passed, and the poor husband finally finished the clothes. The elves all agreed that they looked great.

The next day when he woke up, he discovered rolls of cloth draped all over his house.

Wow! What a surprise!

Many customers came to the shop, and all of them wanted to buy clothes made of the new cloth.

One even said, "If you succeed, I will give you all my gold."

He was overjoyed! He realized that the elves had lived up to their promise.

R obotic aircraft

The pandemic of the century, coronavirus, will occur in 2020, and we will need to be in isolation like a prison. We won't be able to travel to certain countries, either.

And so, I thought, how wonderful it would be to have an aircraft where you could still go where you wanted and there wasn't any need for quarantine.

I hate quarantine!

It's like being in prison!

So, I imagined a new invention of a flying robot that would take me and my mum straight back to China and land quietly in our garden in the dead of night when no one was there.

Dad would be thrilled and surprised to see us suddenly in front of him!

Ha! Ha! Ha! Isn't it exciting? My own science fiction.

Do you want to know about the robot flying the machine I invented?

Well, it can let you travel from one country to another country – just like going on a free holiday. During the lockdown, when airlines are cancelled and people worried, the robot can fly 1500 kilometers a second. It can even go to the planet of aliens.

It can be used during the lockdown, for it has medical energy to cure people on board while flying.

The robot can also two pairs of wings to be self-powering and not in need of any energy source. It even has its own maps – visible when you press G on the side of its head, like Google Maps.

The two buttons on its left leg – A and F – are for Flying and Updating.

My flying fantasy is not that far away in the future. Fasten your seatbelts, we are going on the most enjoyable journey we have ever had!

Story 38

G wendoline's nightmare

"Good morning darling!"

Gwendoline was in her room crying; she didn't know why.

It was midnight and, suddenly, there was a terrible roar and a yell. She looked out the window and saw her parents had been turned to stone, and she was in shock. She decided to go out of their house, and she heard a whisper. She woke up and saw her dad smiling, and she was in surprise.

Her dad said that her mom was on holiday from work and that they should all go and explore a rainforest! Yah!

"I dreamt that you and mum had turned to stone!"

Her dad was still smiling, and the smile never fades.

She went to the bathroom and took a shower. Then, she looked back at the bed where she had just had the nightmare and said to herself: "It was a nightmare!"

She went downstairs and told her dad that she's ready to go exploring.

Story 39

Party Show-off

Britney, Kuala, Nancy, Granita, Josephine, Sarah and Fatima were planning a party inside Hartley's colourful bedroom. They decided they were going to have it in the hall with a disco ball.

"Halo gees! Is ma English improving ah bit?" asked Kuala, who had extra English lessons because she wasn't very good at it.

"Teeny weeny bit," replied Granita, who had a higher score than Kuala. "Ma should be My as ah is just a."

"Ummu… O-o-o-o-okay?" stuttered Kuala for no reason.

Josephine's father and mother entered the room and to deliver some news.

"Kuala, your mother had been sent to the police station. If you want to, you can throw a party. We knew that your mother has always been in a furious temper if your English is, and she doesn't like that you have not been doing your school's homework." replied, "Okay, I am quite sleepy now. But do use my WhatsApp, and tell my friends to meet me at Hartley's Bedroom, okay?"

"I am going to drift off to sleep..." yawned Kuala.

The parents looked at each other and nodded.

"Kuala! Wake up! Wake...UUUUPPPPP!" shouted Jo's Mum & Dad.

"Your friends are...," they began, but Kuala stopped them.

"Here?"

"Yes."

"Okay."

"Now, get up and do some yoga, or video gaming, or even maybe prepare some popcorn! You don't have to, but you always should do your gardening."

"Okay! Thanks!"

Kuala then got up and did some gardening.

Then she went to a party to show-off.

Story 40

My shocking story

Everyone has their likes and dislikes. There will also be animals that are afraid and animals that are not afraid.

There was a girl, whose name is Tina, who was afraid of ducks. She was very frail.

Once when she was in the attic, she saw a door labelled 'pet'. Inside was an iron tank filled with fishes and other kinds of sea creatures. She then found a carboard box with holes in it. She thought it may contain a snake, mole, or any other small pet.

When she peaked through one of the holes, she saw a yellow figure quacking on a marble pool and eating bread. When she opened the box, a duck looked up at her! It quacked, and she screamed.

"Ahh! Please help me! Mum and dad! I can't handle this!"

Her parents rushed upstairs to the attic.

"You called us for nothing, Tina? How dare you!" they shouted.

"What now? Are you allergic or scared of ducks again?"

"Yes, dad dear! I am, said Tina boldly. She thought that she was in big trouble.

"Now, darling. Don't be afraid of ridiculous things - be brave!" her mum said.

"Okay mum," said Tina sadly, weeping loudly.

The Girl in the Photograph

A little girl from the royal family needed a male artist to paint her portrait. The problem was that she would not leave her palace, and the rules of the castle did not allow anyone of the opposite sex to enter.

Her servant suggested taking a picture of the princess with a camera and handing it over to an artist. After considering the suggestion for a while, the princess thought it was a good idea.

One day, a very professional photographer came to the palace. The princess wore a white jacket and a white skirt with lace. She also had thinned her eyebrows and brushed her brown hair.

The photographer thought, "Maybe she should also wear a white ribbon in her hair to look even more beautiful."

After taking many pictures, the photographer was still not satisfied.

The princess felt tired, and she smelled something strange. After the servant left the room, she sat motionless for several minutes. Just then, the servant left the room. She then suddenly shouted,

"I need to go to the Loo! Now!"

The photographer was worried that the princess's dress would be all wrinkled when she came back from the lavatory.

She hoped everything would be okay, as the shoot would only take a few more minutes.

But the princess could not help crying. At last, the servant heard her and ran to help.

The princess said to the servant, "please check what the smell is. I almost choked on the disgusting smell!"

It turned out that the painter had forgotten to cover the pot of paint when he had gone to the lavatory and the smell had drifted around the palace.

Even worse, it turned out that the princess was severely allergic to the smell of paint.

When the painter heard the commotion, he was too frightened to come out of the toilet.

"You get out here!" commanded the servant.

What a disaster photo day turned out to be.

Story 42

Christmas dinner

Tonight, Granger and I decided to create a vegetable pizza from the produce in our garden.

We used cheese, ham, lettuce, bread, and then the nice-smelling roast chicken on the top.

Even though it was rushed, we had three guests - Milli, Harty and Keane – arriving with appetites.

I decided to wash my hands since they were oily, and I was struggling go even properly hold a spoon or a metal rod for fishing!

Milli removed the pudding from the pan - it looked like mud on grass! The green jelly was the base for the chocolate sauce. Harty and I peeped at it, surprised, and we both thought that it looked disgusting.

"We can have some fruit salad if you guys don't want to eat the pudding," Milli suggested after seeing our sour faces, slowly turning light green.

I looked over Keane's shoulder then saw some fruity colors like orange, red or yellow.

I sat back, worried.

What if she was warming her knife over the flames?

After a while, Keane shoved the fruit salad beside me. I gasped and decorated my plate with the fruit.

I began my meal, and it wasn't long until we reached the pudding. I loved the chocolate sauce, so I cut a nice piece of the pudding then shoved it into my mouth.

Yum!

But then I found a piece of hard metal inside the second mouthful.

I asked.

Harty grabbed hold of it and then announced that it was an ancient coin from Greece.

She also said that you could make a wish

at Christmas dinners if you find a coin inside a piece of pudding.

A sparkle lit her eyes.

Writing the haunted house

The spectral moonlight lit my face. A ghostly image shivered through the overgrown hedges, which made a *woo!* Sounds arrived in their weird language.

I stepped forward when I heard a dripping sound. Then it started to rain heavily.

I remembered the time when my nanny told me that every drop of rain can be poison. She explained how she nearly died at the age of five when she swallowed a drop of rain.

"Hello? Anybody here?" I asked, looking around.

"Hello? Anybody here?" I asked again.

I went through the building, tiptoeing across the marble floor. It seemed like a wealthy family had lived here.

There were brownish stains on the floor, guns hung from the walls, spiderwebs, and a hovering skeleton.

The house was covered in all sorts of scary stuff.

I then walked up the blood-red carpeted stairs. *Creeps!* I saw a coffin with knives and swords pushed through the sides, and inside was a skeleton clothed in a man's wedding suit.

Was he murdered or something? Hmm!

I saw a dormitory, and inside were claws on beds, red-black capes, sharp teeth, and bottles of a glowing green potion on each bedside table.

How on earth did they make this? Wow!

When I left the dorm, a shiver ran down my spine. The wooden floor creaked below my feet. I started running as fast as I could. I started asking for help, but no one answered.

Then everything went black.

Hours later.

What?! Is this a town full of visible, see-through ghosts?

I woke up - the haunted mansion was all a dream.

I never went back to that haunted mansion ever again.

Story 44

The missed artistic genius

I'm Noreen S. I'm in year five of a great prep school.

Unfortunately, this year I encountered a super infectious disease that swept the world - coronavirus.

After my Christmas holiday, the school was closed for three months, and I was forced to study online.

My elder sister, who is going off to university this fall, is back with her boyfriend, who's an elder brother who's good at mathematics. They all had to also stay at home for online lessons. Our home was suddenly bursting, and my mother suddenly had a lot of extra housework.

Although there are online classes every day, except Saturday and Sunday, the timetable is not as busy as when we are at school. Therefore, I have more time to do the things I like, such as painting.

Because I like painting so much my mom hired an art teacher to help me.

Every Saturday, the drawing teacher teaches me through the computer. She asked me to call her Spring, which turns out to be her last name. What an artistic expression!

Teacher Spring taught me to use acrylic pens, acrylic paint, watercolours and glitter pens.

She uses two mobile phones to teach me - one allows me to draw pictures, the other lets me video what I'm doing. During the lesson, my mom is like my assistant.

Teacher Spring shows me how the aesthetics of European, Asian and African people are all entirely different.

European eyeballs are lighter in colour than those of Asians and Africans, so they prefer light-colourer paintings. I learned this very quickly.

When my teacher needs me to use a pen, paint, or paper, my mum's always handy.

Saying my mom's name here has a special meaning.

My mom's username means flower in Chinese. And she very much likes flowers, something she wants me to paint. For this reason I have completed some beautiful flower paintings.

But she also likes to give me objects draw at random.

Mom always looks at my paintings patiently and often gave me some strange suggestions.

She cant paint herself, even though when she was a child she liked to draw pictures. My grandfather taught her to draw a cup, but it would often take days to complete. She became tired of it and stopped drawing.

Although my grandfather's interest in painting destroyed my mom, he was a fine artist when he was younger - often drawing works which were dozens of meters wide.

These vast murals are incredible!

Poor mom! If she hadn't been made to sketch those cups she would have been a great artist!

Story 45

Jamie's terrible experience

Jamie got caught in a bad snowstorm when he was skiing in Italy last year. After that, he thought he was seldom coming back.

It had been sunny when he went up that day, and he had no idea that the storm would nearly killed him.

While Jamie was still on the mountain, the pesky snowstorm started. He insisted on skiing down the hill in defiance of his companion's advice.

He was on the last run when suddenly he ran out of ski run and crashed into a gully.

The storm was so fierce that he couldn't see beyond a metre in front of him. Something bad had happened and was just beginning to realise it.

He was hurt and he couldn't get his foot up out of the snow.

A bitter wind began blowing in great flakes of snow. The wind shook the branches while it roared and howled.

Jamie tried to crawl. He was out of breath, and in too much pain to shout for help.

He crawled into a hole beside him to escape from the blizzard. Suddenly he heard a cry, and he felt the hair on his hand.

"Hmmm... A Wolf?" he worried. He thought he was resigned to his fate.

But it was a Saint Bernard that was licking him!

When the storm was over, Jamie realized it was the dog. The dog barked to remind him of the water it had round its neck. Jamie saw the bottle and gulped down the water. He had been so thirsty.

After that, he feels a lot better.

He realised he should not be so stubborn in the future.

That presents the dog

"KNOCK, KNOCK..."

I heard a knock on the door, and I guessed it was my mum's parcel.

"Mum, there's a parcel!" I shouted, but my mum didn't answer me. So, I opened the door.

Someone had left a large cardboard box, with the word Fragile stamped on it. When I opened the box I found a pink bow, a red ribbon with a golden pattern, a golden drinking bowl, another bowl, but sparkly pink, and another cardboard box inside – again labelled FRAGILE?!

Inside this box I found another pink bow, a red ribbon with a golden pattern, a golden drinking bowl, another bowl, but sparkly pink, and another cardboard box, this time labelled, FRAGILE! BE CAREFUL!

I hoped that it wasn't a monster, and it wasn't. It was a cute, fluffy, white dog!

I am crying with pure happiness, and then I took a nap.

Two hours later I woke up with a sudden fright. Oh, it was just the alarm.

I went to my bedroom and saw my dog playing with a dolly. I decided to take the dog with me and decorate it with the decorations. First, I showered it, then I rubbed the dog dry.

I pulled out a ribbon and tied it around the dog's neck. It did look nice on the dog, I am glad.

I poured water in the golden bowl and put dog food in the pink bowl. The dog was starving, and it needed some rest as well.

I introduced the dog to his new sleeping cushion – it was gold and pink. The dog slept well.

"My darling, do you like this little dog?"

I suddenly heard my mum's voice.

"Your birthday is only two days away, so I discussed it with your dad, and we decided to get you a

puppy as a birthday present."

Oh, my gosh! My dream has come true! It turns out this cute dog is my birthday present!

"I like it very much! Mom! Thank you and dad for the birthday present! I will love it as much as you love me. I feel like I'm going to faint with happiness…"

The bully

Kester stepped off the bus and froze.

He saw a group of boys waiting for him, and they were all laughing.

He said, "See, what I'm telling you?"

Lucy crossed her arms.

The boy in the middle of the crowd, shouted, "You're such a fool."

Lucy felt very sad. She had never seen such cruelty towards an innocent boy!

Kester suddenly had an idea! He said, "If we go to that old corral, they won't follow us! They were always afraid of the place."

The old corral was abandoned years ago. As he told Lucy of his plan, they went and hid behind a pile of hay. A group of children passed, but their faces were so pale with fear that their trousers fell to the floor.

As the bullies followed Kester and Lucy into the corral, they saw the head of a dead man.

They don't bully Kester anymore, so Lucy and Kester lived happily ever after that.

Story 48

T hree mini-stories

1. Wendy was cursed

Once, a little girl named Wanda was in her house. She loved to make up stories and read them to her little sister. Her little sister was always asking for just one more, I promise! If you wonder what her little sister's name is, it is Wendy Bake.

Now, Wendy is a reticent girl. She has many friends, just because she doesn't disturb other people's reading time.

Wanda's story made her little sister laugh! This is when things start to go strange.

Wendy usually comes home with a cap on, but today, she wore a scarf. She doesn't carry her own bag but had her friend's shopping bag.

Wanda asked, "Why did you carry that bag?"

Wendy didn't reply, and she was deadly silent.

They went indoors, and they became chattier and chattier.

Wanda suddenly noticed a green spot on her sister's forehead when she took her hat off. She shouted, "Cursed child! Cursed child!"

2. Sweet lemon isn't real

Once in the town of Dudley, a family decided to have some lemonade.

There was Sam, the father, Julie, the mum and Brandon Sky, the child. Mum made some cakes, and dad made the lemonade. Unfortunately, dad mistook sugar for salt and poured it into the lemonade.

At resting time, everybody took a cup of lemonade and started drinking:

"Dad, why is the lemonade so sweet? Please add more salt", said the child.

Dad added more salt, he but made a mistake again! Sky pointed, "Look, mum! Dad is so mistakable!"

Mum sighed - she was thinking the same. She thought Sweet lemonade isn't natural.

3. Why you are... SO HANDSOME?

Mr. Molly wasn't loved by his students, but he was adored by the headmistress.

People from all around the world went to that school, to see him! WHOA! But Miss Sophie, the headmistress, got him first. He chose her to be his wife.

One day, he married Miss Sophie. They went on to have two children.

Marcus, Mr. Molly's brother, became an uncle. And Helix, Miss Sophie's little sister, became an aunty.

They lived contentedly ever after.

If you wonder where the Molly family are, they are in a particle of this page!

The hidden book

Chapter 1

Once upon a time, there was a little girl called Anna. She woke up and did what she was meant to do. Day after day she followed her instructions, until she grew up and became a book writer.

She spent all her time writing books.

After she had written 99 books, she decided she had written her last book.

Day after day passed and her birthday arrived. She looked at the time; 16:34. Still seven and half hours to her birthday!

She was so excited about her birthday. She continued writing her final book, and she was happy that everyone was still buying her books - except her last book.

Her last book had cast a great spell.

Everyone who read it earned £1,000,000! Everyone was surprised, and they don't know how it had happened.

Anna read the great spell, "No Fiona, nation era. Ghiberti."

When Anna was 34 years old, her brother called her to say happy birthday. He also said that Anna had become a great famous person in her hometown.

Chapter 2

Before she left for her trip to Russia, Anna said goodbye to her house and family. She went to the airport, and after going through it, 9 minutes later, she was on the airplane and ready to fly.

After 7 hours and 22 minutes she arrived in Russia.

She is so happy and excited!

When she walked through the airport everyone cheered for her.

She went out in the street and called a taxi so she could visit her adopted mother. Her adopted mother was so happy to see her!

Her adopted mother had purple hair, red lips, golden earrings, dark blue lashes, pink, golden high heels, and a light blue bag.

They had their tea, they walked back to the mother's home, but this time, they walked into their garden.

Chapter 3

The trip ended and Anna returned to her book.

She had hidden the book because she thought that it contained a great spell.

The end!

Story 50

The magic shining black cloak

I stepped into the mist-shrouded, open, dark woodland, where the crooked branches are rarely bare.

At first, I felt like I was being followed, walking into this haunted, scary, dark forest with no lights and hardly anything to see except ghosts.

I was so scared that I thought I wouldn't be able to find my way out, so I felt lost. Suddenly, I saw a black thing moving in the thin, hazy air. I took a closer look; it was a black clock that made me warm when I went close!

I grabbed it and hung it on my back. An extraordinary thing happened. I found myself floating in the air. I could no longer see the ground or the trees.

I'm flying, but I can't see anything. Suddenly, I notice a ray of light in the distance, coming closer and closer. It's a car. I see a girl get out of the vehicle.

Oh, my God, I recognized the girl. That was my mother when I was a baby. I landed beside the car excitedly.

She is almost the same age as me, but I know she is my mother. I Had travelled back in time.

I excitedly told her, "I am your future daughter!"

She looked at me in surprise. I know I had scared her. Unfortunately, I didn't have any gifts for her. I told her, I will come back to you tomorrow; I will bring you toys you have never played with and snacks you have never eaten.

So, I put on the clock cloak, took off again, and went home.

The next day, I prepared to go to my mother's childhood.

I was bringing things that didn't exist in her day. Her friends were curious about me. But she kept my secret for me.

Zaria and her new dog

Once upon a time, there lived a girl called Zaria. She was neither rich nor poor but was perfect in many ways.

Her cousin is an orphan, and Zaria's family chose her cousin to live with them. Zaria didn't like her much because she still wore her old pink sweatshirt.

The cousins sat down to breakfast and enjoyed corn and chicken, as well as some chocolate and sweetmeat.

Here I say, why are you all being so dull?

Now I warn, these horrible crooks, who you haven't noticed yet, might kill you!

Now, these crooks were neither competent nor clever enough to escape from the strong policemen.

Quickly, the policemen captured them because he noticed their smelly pee on the floor. Imagine that! Stinky pees mean that you are easily spotted.

Now you know all about the smelly thieves, we need to talk about Zaria.

Her new dog is called Wager.

You would imagine that this would be exciting because Zaria had never owned a dog before.

And she wants to hug him, but it was too dusty because the dog needs a bath. A bath with bubbles so it would be nice to let him know that they loved him much than ever!

The dog cost £2,557 - it was worth it, though, believe me.

Story 52

The Magic Wishing Tree two

Intro: Three confident kids are climbing an enchanted tree. Susan, the naughty, bossy, childish girl is leading them.

"Wow! Elves and fairies!" shouted Matilda.

"Shut up, Matilda," said Peter.

They decided to climb the grand tree and see who's living there. Climb and climb - they almost reached the top, but Susan was tired.

"Ahh...let's go down because I'm tired," she complained.

"No, you can't. That's too high to fall - and climbing downwards is not easy," the other children told her.

"How do you go down?" Susan asked.

"No idea," they responded.

Susan began to cry.

Just then a door opened.

"What's all that noise? I can't sleep!" a Candy-faced man said.

"Are you a Candy which has a b..." began Matilda, but Peter stopped her.

"You can ride on my slider if you give me a candy of any kind," began the candy-faced man, "do you have any?"

The legend is that if he eats candies, his face will grow more handsome.

"No," replied Susan Buttercup.

"What is on the top of the tree? Candy?" asked Susan.

"You can call me Candy," said the Candy Man.

"The take-what-you-want-land is going to be on top tomorrow - but please make me some candies tomorrow if you want to slide on my slider today, ok?" he continued

"Ok," the children agreed.

And that's how the girls and the boy solved the matter of Susan being so bossy.

The Party

I go to the hotel, and my friends were going to follow on soon. I reached the information desk where there were lots of party balloons and stuff.

"Lola, are you here? Call the others if you are!" I shouted.

After 10 minutes I finally heard a reply.

"Yes, I am here, the others will arrive at lunch for we need to set things out."

"Like what?" I asked, my heart pounding.

"Just thingies," she replied.

I went to the information desk to sign with my account.

This is one of those hotels that needs people to sign to make sure that they aren't aliens or scary creatures.

I went to the kitchen door where I saw a stool with a key and bell on the top.

I pressed the bell and…

RING! RING! RING!

"Lola, bring Mrs. Eliana and Mr. Sonnet to the table! Bring the others in as well!" I shouted, as the waiter brought in the food.

Then we had a delicious meal.

Story 54

S uspicious Miss Smith

Maria and Mary are sisters and they both have green eyes. But their hair is not the same colour. Maria's hair is tawny but dyed pink.

She usually likes to wear a bow on her head at Easter but puts a Christmas hat on at Christmas. The other sister, Mary, was much bolder. Mary has black hair, but she is always rude to Miss Smith.

The neighbours always called Miss Smith "the permanent worker".

Miss Smith is lovely to Mary every day!

"Who's stolen my watch?" asked Miss Smith.

"Not me! It's Maria! She did it!" said Mary, which made Maria sad and unhappy.

"No, no, it was not me!" she stammered.

"Come, follow me!" Miss Smith, suddenly feeling very uncomfortable about a hole in her mouth.

She told Maria that she needed to see a dentist first.

Maria was kind enough to take Miss Smith to the dentist. They stood in the dentist's line.

Then she became impatient. When it finally came to her turn, she saw sharp tools, white walls covered with model mouths, first aid kits and bags, and a cabinet.

She was frightened by what she saw.

She turned to run but was grabbed by the nurse.

"Sit down, because if you run, I will hold open your mouth."

Miss Smith sat down and did as she was told, but she tried to shout while the doctor was operating. Maria was surprised by her reactions. Miss Smith had always struck her as brave.

Maria could not help laughing at Miss Smith being afraid of the dentist.

When Maria laughed, Miss Smith realised it was Mary who had stolen her watch.

What a strange mind!

Mary was beaten and locked in a cupboard for a week.

Story 55

The devil boy

They have the best prep school in lake city. But a strange thing happened today at 3:45 p.m., when the girls and boys in year four were playing hockey with another school.

In the school's old and mysterious tree-climbing area, a UFO suddenly appeared. The boys and girls stared at the never-before-seen aircraft in amazement. The teachers stopped working.

Then the UFO landed in the tree, and unexpectedly lowered a floating metal ladder. Finally, the aliens, like we see in the movies, appeared with a human.

"That's Ethan, my former classmate!" yelled Noz Song. The ten-year-old girl's classmates were surprised that she knew the guy with the alien.

And it was clear from his appearance that he was also from Asia.

"Cool!" yelled Hugo; one of the year fives in the crowd. He must have thought it would be cool to ride a UFO with an alien.

At this moment, the alien walked straight up to Noz.

"Remember him? What a naughty devil with glints in eyes, and red horns with an arrow-shaped tail!" it said.

Noz quickly realised that this was the same alien who gave her the coronavirus drug recipe.

It is **AITE TYI**.

"Of course, I remember him! He used to bully me! And often he was with the other naughty boys who would bully the girls!" Noz said.

"I'm going to take him to our planet, because I know he'll grow up to be a monster! I have brought him here first because I want him to apologise." **AITE TYI**, before taking Ethan to Noz.

"That's incredible, you have alien friends!" the other children shouted. "And it's getting justice for you!"

Noz knows that her classmates will never know how hateful and disgusting Ethan was.

"Why don't his parents discipline him?" they asked.

Hugo, who was a little afraid of aliens, couldn't help asking silly questions.

"I guess his parents are nouveau riche. Indeed, they don't know how to teach their kids," said Noz's classmate, Sahara.

"It would be a cool way to get to another planet," said Hugo, who looked as though he was longing to also go to the mysterious planet.

"Can't he ever return to Earth? Will he never see his parents again? Can they make video calls?" they enquired.

"That's for sure," **AITE TYI** answered.

Suddenly, Noz felt sorry for Ethan.

"May I make a request?" she asked.

"Tell me, and I'll see if I can do it!" **AITE TYI** instructed. **It** seemed to know what she was thinking.

"If he's going to be better off on your planet, could he have a weekly video call with his parents? And if he continues to get better, could he be allowed to go back to his home on Earth once every term?" she asked.

"Oh, if you put it that way, I'll think about it," **AITE TYI** answered her.

"Ethan, please apologise to Noz quickly!" he continued. "A sincere apology! Not the duplicitous kind of apology! Look ashamed!"

Ethan's face went red, and the guy who had never told anyone he was sorry before didn't know how to say it. He stood there like a tree.

At last, he bowed to Noz. His voice was like a mosquito's whisper.

"I'm sorry that I used to bully you. It's my fault. I'll never do it again."

AITE TYI waited for him to finish and took him to the spaceship.

Soon the spaceship released a variety of colours of rings as it rose into the air.

Then, five seconds later, it was gone entirely.

The story of girls Nancy and Rowley

There were two children; one called Nancy and the other called Rowley. They are friends.

Nancy has three sisters: Tracy, Sassy, and Connie.

Nancy also has a brother, who is called Rory. She has also lost her dog.

Rowley has no sisters, but she has eight brothers. Her mum went in a fury one day, and out came the eight babies. They were just like eight potatoes rolling out of a bag. No one knows why the mum was angry.

Here is a list of their families.

NANCY: Eight years old and half a month. Doesn't use the left hand. Brown straight hair. Green eyes.

TRACY: Twelve years old and two months. Doesn't use the right hand. Golden curly hair. Blue eyes.

SASSY: Thirteen years old with no months. Doesn't use the right hand. Brassy plaited hair. Blue eyes.

CONNIE: Nine years and seven months. Doesn't use the left hand. Purple-blue flowed hair with no hairbands. Blue eyes.

RORY: Twenty-one years old with one month. Don't use the left hand. A very short blue died hair. Blue eyes.

You now know all the members of Nancy's family. Their surname is BURTON.

Let's look some more at the families and we can then tell the whole story!

Rowley's dad is a VIP taxi driver, and her mom is a BOOKSELLER.

Let's go on! Do not stop reading this fascinating story with all its magical adventures!

ROWLEY: Eight years and five months. Doesn't use the left hand. Brown hair. Green eyes.

No one is sure how old Rowley's brothers are.

Once in the morning, Rowley saw a whoosh of wood colour. He was so confused. He just saw a chair, that suddenly came whooshing by…

"Hang on, what's that?" thought Rowley.

"Ok, I am not reporting this to those baddies, the reporters, as they blab and giggle all the time"

Then the chair landed with a bump right in front of her! Then Rowley sat in it and went on many further adventures with Nancy.

THE END

Story 57

T he Journalists

Chapter 1: Upon the rock pool

"Do you feel like anything today, Gwendoline? I'm going to the highway in my car. Dad's going to drive, and mum is going to bring up turkey sandwiches. You are going, aren't you?" I asked, feeling for the chocolates in my pocket.

"Yes, only if you have at least three chocolates to take," Gwendoline replied, as she turned away to face the telly.

Mum arrived with ham sandwiches in paper bags - a sandwich for each person. She had also filled up the water bottles, packed some desserts such as chocolates and some fruit.

"We're leaving here in about... wait, 15 minutes. Pack, Gwen! Quick! Or the rock-pool centre will be closed, and our visiting appointment is today!"

"Fine, but I'm going to the loo first," she he replied, thumping upstairs.

"Okay, but hurry"

After a while, Gwen came back downstairs with a pink bag in her hands.

Soon, dad and mum waved for us to get in the car, with Gwen sulking on the way.

A few minutes later...

"Have we arrived yet? I'm so bored," moaned Gwen, who had turned purple.

Mum replied, "Soon, darling! Oh, and you too, my honeysuckle!"

"You always say that mummy!"

"Take your manners seriously and respect your mum," I said, squinting my eyes to look like I am angry and annoyed.

"Fine! Ugh!" replied Gwendoline.

"What a f..." muttered Gwen.

"What DID YOU SAY? A SWEAR WORD AGAIN?" I half-shouted and half asked, like I can read her mind.

"Shh...Gwen... You'll have a code red again! Oh, my cod..." shushed mum to Gwendoline.

Gwendoline had an annoyed look on her face; twisted mouth, lowered eyebrows, small looking eye-shields, and then she rolled her eyes.

"Ooh, yes, we're here!" shouted mum.

"But unfortunately, we are in the last available class - no rockpool for us, sorry!"

"Yay!!!" shouted Gwen.

"Shh! Code red!" responded mum while lowering her head to make her eyes more prominent.

One long walk later...

"There yet?" Gwendoline asked again.

"Yes..." replied mum, with a twisted mouth, as we reached a blue hut beneath a rickety cliff.

We entered a corridor. When we reached the end of the hall, there was a sign "Register your time here, please wait if there is a queue. Many thanks, manager," blocking our way.

"Kay? This look weir..." began Gwen, but

mum stopped her by silencing her.

Gwen kicked the walls repeatedly, which aroused a man with a 'Manager' badge, who appeared at the counter.

"Finally! B..." began Gwen, while skipping and hopping. But mum pulled her back by the skirt and whispered; "Shh...Enemies are coo..."

I stopped her.

"Give her a break. Let her play. You keep saying that and pulling her back like you're a VILLAIN!

"Keep calm and everything will be fine. Ok, mum?" I continued.

"Yyyyyes honeysuckle!" she responded. Mum had never been called a villain before, so she stuttered along the rocky way.

Chapter 2

The glimpses and boring jokes

We passed the pools, where the numbers of each pool and which class was in it was displayed.

Jealous-looking people passed by; some of them snitching or telling stories while others were telling jokes.

We then reached our pool, with the number 209 on a bronze post.

A coconut tree was on the right, with an empty crab shell hanging on the front.

Then Helen, who is my friend, showed up and was allowed to enter my rock pool.

Then Beatrice, Monica, Kayla and Matilda also arrived after Helen.

"What is named Shirley but is in prison?" asked Kayla with a chuckle on her face.

"Anne Shirley the character in a book, sillies! Ha! Good one, isn't it? Hahaha..." laughed Kayla loudly, making the people in cabin 208 angry and hot-tempered.

"Oh, please! No more jokes! I feel sick!" shouted Helen, but Monica continued the jokes.

"Ok, so... What goes up but never comes down?" asked Monica.

"Bread?" Asked Kayla.

"No, Kayla! Bread can't fly, silly," laughed Beatrice.

"Oh, yes, Beatrice!" answered Kayla.

"No, it isn't," muttered Matilda, a teeny-weeny bit loudly.

"You got it! Continue!" shouted Monica while punching the sky.

"Age?"

"YESSSSSSSSS!"

"What? Butttt..."

"No buts! Ha, ha, ha..."

"Wait- did you see that?"

"Nope, not at all...."

Chapter 3

A fish, a duck, and a turtle

"Look, over there is a fish! There is a duck? There's even a turtle here! This must mean something important…," Monica pointed to a patch of water far away.

But then, a servant in a fancy suit came over and asked what we would like to eat.

"Some healthy fruit and ice cream, please! Thanks very much! Have a good day too!" answered mum.

The servant nodded, then left.

Nine minutes later, the same servant came back with a basket of fruit and seven ice lollies.

"Wow! Gracias!" shouted Monica, since she's Spanish, but he'd gone before she remembered to speak.

"Weird man," she thought. "That man must have a secret recipe up his sleeve!"

An hour later…

"The sun's too bright!" moaned Gwen

She opened her little pink bag and got out a pair of sunglasses.

"Ahh- that's better. No distractions – the brightness can't blind my eyes anymore."

"Wow! This duck looks like a flower, and this fish looks like a pointy creature, and this turtle... oh, is normal.

"Let me see if I can find these creatures on Google. Oh, I see... all of these, except this turtle, come from China."

"Now, what does it say? These animals are rare, and don't often breed. I see! What?! five more fishes, six more flowery ducks, and eight more turtles! So cool!

"Wow, I must tell them this! Guys! These animals came from China and had to swim miles and miles to get here!"

"Look! One is about to speak," interrupted Helen.

"I am hungry, sir! Is food available?" asked a fish.

"Yes. According to my silver fins, we have finally arrived at a beach...

at San Sebastián." replied a bigger fish with silver fins.

"Hello, fishes! We can buy you some Spanish seafood paella! Want some?" asked Matilda.

"Yes, yes, yes, yes, yes, yes, yes, yes!" sang the fish gang."

"There are also churros if you wish," she added.

"Yes, yes, yes, yes, yes, yes, yes, yes…" the fish continued singing.

"We come from the Yangtze River, and we came here for the seafood," they explained.

30 minutes later…

"Our next stop is to the UK to watch the football championships! Can you take us there?"

"Yes!"

"Food, food, food, food, food, food, food, food!" shouted the gang.

Chapter 4:

Watching the European Football Championships

"Here it goes— look at them, fishes!" cried the leader of the fishes.

"Italy is winning! Boo! Boo! Go England!" shouted Misty, a purple-finned fish.

"Yeah, go, England! Go Britain and go the UK!"

"I disagree!" shouted a silver finned fish, and then everybody, including the people, looked shocked, and their faces went pale.

"Just saying, you guys should say: Go silver! Go silver! Go...SILVER!"

Then a person shouted, "Go Rashy! Go go go!"

"No, it needs correcting!" remarked Silver, the bossy fish, who added: "It should be

go silver! Go go go!"

"Nope, I won't change it!"

"Yeah! I agree!"

"Agree!"

"Agree!"

"Delete all this nonsense! I have a different way of playing football, you see! First, freeze the goalkeeper with ice powers then kick the ball into the goal. See?" shouted a hockey referee in the crowd.

"London Bridge is falling, falling, falling..." repeated Misty, the purple finned fish. Then, all the fishes, except Silver began, to sing too!

Silver just crossed his arms and put on his Money-shaped-sunglasses. He looked hilarious!

Story 58

Travelling on a plane

Three girls, named Lily, Barbara and Maple, were holding their tickets in the middle of the airport, looking confused.

"Where are we going?" asked 10-year-old Maple, who is the youngest of the three.

"To A3, to put our luggage. I've got your passports," replied Lily, who had located the A3 table.

The girls queued up and soon found themselves at the front. The staff member asked for their passports. Lily's black American Tourister was placed onto the heaver. Maple's Unicom suitcase, which was light, and Barbara's purple lightweight bag, that has a musical note on it, followed.

"Lily, when are we going on the plane?" asked the tired-looking Barbara.

"Soon," replied Lily, who now has an annoyed look.

The three girls then went to the gate to wait.

"Whoa! This is so cool!" shouted Barbara and Maple, who saw a wall full of rhombuses in rainbow coloured order.

"Can I have one in my bedroom?" Barbara asked Lily.

"Yes, but it has to be small so that it fits," remarked Lily.

The girls were the first in the queue! Wow!

"Yay!" shouted Maple and Barbara together as they ran up the corridor that leads to the plane. In front of the aircraft stood a man wearing a black suit with a white shirt.

"Here is the ticket and passport, sir," said Lily.

But the man her ignored her and signalled for her to go forwards to hand it in.

Lily did as she was told, and she got on her seat, numbered 101. She put the two items of luggage onto the overhead cabins.

Lily then put tags onto the empty seat next to her. "This trip will only take nine hours, and Maple will want to sleep," she thought.

"Okay, Lily?" Maple said as she arrived.

"Here's your iPad," offered Lily to Barbara.

Maple was soon asleep.

"Du du du..." hummed Barbara as she watched her iPad.

Lily told her to be quiet and not disturb Maple.

A staff member told everybody that the plane was going to land in the water, so everybody was to put on their yellow life jackets.

A yellow slide was put outside the plane. Everybody slid down the slide and, it made a whooshing sound.

Lily, Barbara and Maple held their luggage as they slid down too!

They then continued their journey to Thailand by boat.

Story 59

The Family Easter Vacation

"Candy, Tommy and Noreen, come here at once! We've got an event just for you guys; you'll love it!" shouted mum. She was in the kitchen baking chocolate cookies.

"Okay, mum!" they all replied as they rushed into the kitchen.

"Alright, now... Tommy, play with the things you want, meanwhile I will talk to Candy and Noreen about Easter and about the chocolate matter."

"Ok, mum!" shouted back Tommy, as he went back to his video-gaming.

"So, Noreen and Candy, I am sure that you will like this. Today, we are doing an egg hunt! A chocolate one, in fact! Love it?"

"Yes!"

"Good! Now... let's do it!" They then went to the garden and Noreen caught a glimpse of three eggs!

169

She raced to grab all of them. One was blue with orange dots, one was green with yellow stripes, and the last one was pink with a red heart on it!

Then Candy found two eggs - one was aqua with a letter 'C', and the other one was a yellow one but with an 'M' on it.

Noreen then found another pink egg, but this time with an 'N' on it.

"Six eggs are hidden. I see that you've found them all," said mum. "Come and eat or save them here while you chump on the chocolate cookies!"

The End.

Fantastic Poems

1.The Odd Mushroom

The odd mushroom,

that's bright yellow green,

it curls around the person,

that goes near.

The odd mushroom,

that does its tricks,

flips around,

And flip flip flip!

The odd mushroom,

that doesn't have stems,

ordinary mushrooms ask,

and ask, ask, ask.

2. The King Parrot

The king parrot,

that's very strong.

Stands on its claws,

without its guts touching the ground.

The king parrot,

that's very handsome.

everyone tries to find him,

And will fail, fail, fail.

3.The Jelly Jumper

The jelly jumper,

looks cosy at sight,

worn on the first Christ night.

With Santa,

with Canta,

with loop,

and with hoop,

People play,

as they may.

Eat dessert daily.

But not too much,

with such a such.

They may,

they make way.

But impossible,

but not too impossible.

Wear the jelly jumper,

that looked cosy at sight.

Worn by the guardian on the night of Christ!

The jumpy jelly,

flops on belly,

really Nelly.

Such a floppy,

much as Poppy.

That sacrifice.

Oh mice.

With care.

Have some Horse mare,

you may,

make way,

of the nature,

with culture,

of the breadcrumbs,

with the tower crumbles.

That jelly took the mess,

with the rest…

The jumpy jelly,

that is jumpy.

It flips around,

and lands flashy.

The jumpy jelly,

that is QUICK,

it helps you,

to finish crafts.

The jelly jumper,

was such a bumper.

It has bumps,

as well as jumps!

You might as well by a quest.

The jelly is to be eaten by a guest.

The jelly to be shaped,

and as well it won't

The jumpy jelly,

that was never a telly.

My, my, my,

such a fly.

If I need a rusty pan,

give me that nasty fan!

Nelly, Nelly, Nelly,

can I play your jumpy jelly?

Keep your hands away from Jim,

for It's way too dark and dim.

Jim is my jelly jumper.

He's a beginner at being a bumper!

Oh dear,

my meaty deer.

The jumpy jelly is making a mess.

The jelly also makes a salad mess.

Yes, yes, yes,

oh, mess, mess, mess!

4. The Beauty of White

The Beauty of white,

that was such a nigh.

The person of gay,

as might light led the way.

You can't stop and stare.

As trotted by a mare,

the beauty of white,

you're so bright!

Reflect your light,

from your sister of bright.

The brightest star,

that was lighter than mar.

As a gift,

you do need a lift,

178

To set out your sibling.

to make them shining!

5. Hop Hop Hop!

Hop, hop, hop,

Bop, bop, bop.

Don't jump too high,

or you may thy!

Chew, chew,

Shoo, shoo.

Don't shoo the rabbit away,

or they will go a long way.

As you jump,

there will be bumps!

6. **Bloom it!**

Part I:

Bloom all you can,

as you will bloom it off.

Where you will shelter.

Where rain never lands.

Don't get deserted,

or you will be dry.

You won't have water then,

and you will never grow.

Find a place then rest for a night,

then find your water and soak it up.

The more water the better.

But not too much.

Too much might lead to,

becoming very like a sea.

Just soak up the extra,

and then have some peace.

Have all your peace,

where a monkey won't ruin it.

For it is nature,

that you just wanted!

Part II

How delicate it is,

for the rabbits.

But don't spoil their view,

just have a look.

You might notice,

that you will see colour.

Not just any kind,

but a special kind.

182

Have one right now.

For it might be available.

It is somewhat tiny,

but very, very, very precious!

7.The striped cat

The striped cat,

that's very naughty,

grabs your socks,

and scratches them.

The striped cat,

that's not well,

coughed very hard,

and sneezed through.

The striped cat,

that's very cute,

touches your hand,

And sleeps calmly.

The striped cat,

that's not good,

scratched your powder,

and jumps around.

8.The special almond tart

The special almond tart,

that smells very nice,

that is very colorful,

that is very eatable.

The special almond tart,

that is very tasty,

that has splashy cream,

that is 'enormously' short.

9. The yellowish rattlesnake

The yellowish rattlesnake,

eats healthy tree-leaves.

Eats your carrots,

and curls up.

The yellowish rattlesnake,

curls around.

Curls around stone,

and sleeps deep.

10. On the way home

On the way home,

don't walk and moan.

For walking will bring us good,

all day long!

You walk past the trees,

you walk past the lake.

You stare at the sun,

and you bring out a bun

11. Super Mum!

Super Mum.

She'll hum, hum, hum.

She's very intelligent.

She's also good.

She does all the chores,

and helps me study.

And makes me a nice pizza,

when I'm hungry!

I love my mum,

She is yum, yum, yum.

She's like a delicious cake;

a never-ending one!

12. Super-Duper Daddy

Super-duper daddy,

that always hugs me.

What he's to be?

An employer?

A jigsaw puzzle?

He's sometimes a muzzle.

He's very funny.

When I never see a bunny!

I love him,

He's never dim.

He's also a photographer

That goes to the upper!

13. My Family!

My Sister the talker.

My Brother the gamer.

My Mother the hugger.

My Father the hummer.

They all have jobs,

but not all are real.

For my Daddy's job,

was to be real.

My mother's real job.

Whenever anyone goes to the knob,

she views the camera,

to see if a thief is there!

14. Monsters

Monsters can be cool,

and some may drool.

Some may have claws,

and some break the laws.

Some may breathe fire,

but some are allergic to wire.

Some may look common,

when people shout 'come-on!'

Some may have X-ray vision,

watching you, watching television!

15. Every Flower's Life

First of all,

comes out a bud.

Then it lands on some mud.

The rains then pour,

as the buds snore...

And second of all,

the bud grows a tail.

But it doesn't get any mail.

The rains then pour,

As the buds snore...

Third of all,

The bud sheds its old skin,

but it isn't made of strong tin.

The rains then pour,

As the saplings snore...

On the fourth day,

the sapling became a tree.

Now it is a grown adult!

16. My Family II

My super mummy,

that gave birth from her tummy.

She does all the chores,

And suffers some bores.

My super-duper daddy,

who never does a maddy.

He may do some music,

… a disc that would never hurt a fiddle.

A 4D game maker,

never to be a baker.

Here goes a basket,

but never a casket.

A great, great chatter,

From a female mad hatter.

195

Great rock music,

would just catch her attention.

17. **Christmas**

Oh, Merry Christmas,

Never, ever can you…

even in war,

cancel the fun.

Hop, hop, hop,

with a game of bop,

enjoy all you want,

but don't be spoiled.

A chicken it may be.

Can be boiled.

All you want is candy,

but don't get Mandy.

Loop, hoop, boop,

play all the games.

A boy named James,

has got a loop.

At the eve,

Santa's sewing the sleeve.

C'ause it's broken.

It has to be new.

Bang, chatter, bang,

the fireworks are out.

Play, play play,

there's even more clay.

Merry…

Christmas! Yay!

18. Everything

Some grass,

some brass,

some water,

some minerals.

Some wood,

some leaves,

some snow,

and some network.

Everything's,

got a thing.

Friends are made,

while others are ruined.

Children are born,

while others turned to mud.

All its ashes,

rise up to the sky.

Wood is cut down,

you are hurting God.

For he made this world,

It's not really ours.

19.The Summer Holidays

You go to the beach,

and eat a peach,

Took a swim and had some ice cream.

You play beat,

as you raise the heat,

and you baked the meat!

You went to the beach,

And then the theatre.

Not so quiet yet,

As there's more to be seen!

Did you bake a bean?

Or have been very keen?

Or took a ride,

on little pony, Reen?

You can watch some play,

or even roll some clay,

or maybe watch a relay!

Or spend your time in books,

reading about some crooks,

but don't get spooked!

20. For Saka, Rashford, and Sancho

Well done Saka!

Scoring through the field…

Never-the-less you win,

and never to be sad.

You'll soon calm down,

and you'll fill up again,

with energy.

You'll win next time.

Well done, Rashford,

Your team is the best.

Rush forward, pick up the ball,

and kick it very far.

No worries. No sadness.

All long, long gone.

And score up, up,

More than 10.

Well done, Sancho!

Driving them all mad.

Enjoy, score, and never do give up,

and beat the keeper's hands.

Go on, win, and never be hurt,

Score, score, till it's 9 or 10!

Be happy, be joyful,

And find out yourself.

21.The world

Over the seas,

in a pirate ship,

while eating your peas,

while touching your gold.

In the heated dessert,

skipping in glee.

Sand was stuck,

To your right knee!

Hunting in the forest,

with bow the third.

By not skipping at all,

you killed a bird.

In the mountains,

in the cave,

with your husband,

whose named Dave!

Seeing so much damage,

ruins every week.

Looks like a week's wage.

But then you climbed the volcano.

Where north always shone,

is the hard bitter winter.

Singing in your tone,

is not a good idea!

Snow, snow, snow,

lines on the lake.

Show, show, show,

Then do your thing!

22.Lego!

Lego, lego,

how I wish for a house.

Lego, lego,

how I want a blouse.

Lego, lego, how I wish for a garden,

That has the sign, 'Marden'!

Lego, lego,

how I want some drama.

Lego, lego,

how I want a pink lama,

Lego, lego, how I want my bedroom,

To have a miniature bathroom!

In the city,

huts and shuts,

coffees and teas,

chips and peas.

Everything you want,

made from blocks,

like even colours,

to make a pink monkey.

A pink monkey,

that exists with yellow wood.

Blue hair and hairy guitars,

blocky buildings and plastic fires.

Mini babies,

turquoise needles,

no wounds,

no shouting,

and no aliveness!

23. A journey on the train.

Faster than fairies, faster than gnomes,

bridges, ditches, buildings and homes.

And charging along like troops in a battle,

while you are feeding the horses and cattle.

All of the sights of the hill and plain,

fly as thick as driving rain.

And again, in the wink of an eye

oiled stations whistle by.

24. Fruit

Look in the basket,

where you'll see some fruit.

And that's what we are gonna talk about today.

In the basket,

there's a red ripe fruit.

It's smooth and crunchy.

But what it is?

An apple!

Beside the apple,

there's a skinny long thing,

What it is, is a banana!

Dragon fruit, strange!

Lychee, bursting!

Blueberries, wow!

Raspberries, pop star!

Strawberries, oh cola!

Orange, common!

25.All seasons (haiku)

In the spring,

flowers grow and sing,

and shrubs grow and defend.

Beaches lay down,

gardens being tend,

Easter soon ended.

In the autumn,

skies darken and crows grow.

A portal to the melancholy world

is ready.

In the winter,

people entered the world.

Snowmen were built and

Christmas came.

Prose collection

1.The star of Spring

On a cold, frosty morning, the sun was hung low in the bright, blue sky. Winter was over, and flowers began to grow in the spring garden. The freezing frost and snow melted by the roaring ball of fire; the sun.

Rowling, my younger brother, stepped cautiously into his wellington boots; and went outdoors. Twigs snapped, flown flowers sprout. Nothing can be more grateful than nature itself. He jumped into the mud-puddle; he got his Wellington boots dirty again!

The night of that day, when he jumped into the mud, the moon glistened. And I was having my stroll when he scared me. The lake right beside me had a wave; it was like it was wanting me to go near it and swim for some time...

My ears tickled, I myself giggled.

My brother was behind me; he used a pigeon feather...

2.The searing of Summer

Part 1

Cool summer days at the beach

Warm sun in the sunny summer sky beats down on my exposed legs, clobbered with sunscreen. Summer was not, my favorite season. But at moments like these, nothing could be better. Resting on my beach chair I observed the wide expanse of chaos. The cloudless day was perfect. The light blue sky was brilliant against the green waves. It felt so picture perfect!

Dashing into the waves I would soak myself in the cool water. Floating in the current as the waves pushed and pulled me in all directions.

Joining in to play beach volleyball with my family, I would jump up to hit the ball. The volleyball would go spinning through the air, water droplets flying off it in all directions, as it swerved in an arc of white and contacted with my mom's arms, locked together in a platform. The ball would ricochet off her arm, shooting sky high. The game would go on like that for a while. Eventually my team would win.

I would frolic in the water, enjoying the day. Splashing water around with my sister. Finally, I would walk along the beach, searching for seashells.

I would find the perfect seashell; a beautiful swirl that wasn't chipped. To make this day even better I might find a sand dollar. A whole one, that's a pearly white colour.

This would qualify to be a perfectly awesome summer day.

Part II

The blistering summer of June and July

June and July roll around, and the season begins to change. The plants grow bloomy, and the sound of cicada is deafening. Summer comes! There's no reason for me to lay in bed on Sunday afternoon. So, without hesitation, I head for the beach to embrace my lovely summer.

Hearing the call of nature, I run towards the sea. When I step on the tiny warm sand, I feel the grains of sand squish slowly through my toes. I can easily find myself in the prominent spot along the crashing white waves. The waves are the brisk children who you cannot resist. They jump and dance in beautiful states and rhythms. I slump down on the sticky sand surround myself in salty water, allowing the foamy mist from the ocean to spray on my face.

The boys around me are playing seesaw with each other, floating up and down along the current. Above me, the clear blue sky doesn't have a single cloud to block the rays of the enthusiastic sun. The rays tickles my eyelids through the sunglasses, and I smile in appreciation of the powerful nature.

I take a little break on the long rows of salt-stained rocks that extend far out into the sea. It's not difficult to find tiny crabs crawling slowly across the gaps. Starfishes lie arbitrarily on the lichen to sunbathe under the rampant fireball. The penetrating heat emanated from the sky wraps around my skin like a warm blanket on a cold winter's night. Once the cool breeze passes by, it evaporates the droplets on my boiling skin.

My brilliant dress blows in the wind like an elegant princess's would. I ease away from the sun's intense heat, which makes me feel much more relaxed.

People from all walks of life enjoy their summer on their way to the beach. Footprints in all sizes, some are small, and some are huge, spread over the sand. It is undoubtedly a fantastic place for a family day. The colorful, outstretched canopies are standing at each corner of the beach for families to have fun.

Sounds of laughter ring into my ears, which makes me feel itchy. There is a smell of sunscreen pervading the atmosphere; it mixes with the evaporating sweat to create an extraordinary odor. A sharp red lifeboat is left at the bottom of the white observation tower, standing by to help the lifeguards complete their mission.

The sun is setting, and the birds are flying by the skyline. The sound of waves sings like my mum humming the lullaby to me; soft and cozy.

All these bring a sense of peace and harmony. My eyelids begin to feel heavy, and the edges of the blue sky become blurred with the sea full of glittering waves. My sweet dream starts.

Part III

The hottest day of July

This hot day in summer is sultry and scorching. It is full of perspiration. One wishes for a cold bath again and again. But even then, there is no rest or respite.

The sultry air is nauseated, and the heart is heaved. The sun in the sky was bright and hot. It's burning like fire. Yes, it is a flaming fireball. It feels like the earth is dry. Day and night, a hot wind blew in the air.

It was the month of July. It was the hottest day of the season. Yet, from early morning, the wind was silent and motionless — the trees and plants were unmoving and stationary.

The leaves on the trees drooped in the sun. Birds and animals panted in the jungle under the branches and trees. The scorching heat continued. The sun is getting hotter. The summer weather has become intolerable. Even the walls and floors were burning. Don't touch anything. Everything is too hot.

It's noon. Like a giant oven, the sun is overhead, and people on the road are turning into potato chips.

One drank water again and again, but still, one was dissatisfied. Ice and cold water were in much demand. But they could not provide any comfort to these irritating bodies. The bazaars were not humming with any activity at all.

They were wearing a cloak of sickness and suffocation. Fans and coolers were of little help, and they were only giving hot air.

This air proved too stiff. A few minute's walk on the road was highly uncomfortable.

By the evening, there was a little respite from the heat. The temperature of the day came down a little. People began to move in the bazaars and on the roads. They wanted to finish their daily chores. But to their bad luck, the light is tripped. Suffocation increased again. Everyone was helpless. They passed the hottest day.

Part IV

Shoreline in Summer

Summer is the perfect time for individuals to visit and enjoy the amazing scenes along the coast.

In addition, the feelings and experiences felt on the beach during the summer are always fantastic.

The beach appears to be alive and joyful with the presence of natural vegetation. There are evergreen plantations along the sands. Images of buoyant seaweeds can be seen along the shore. Palms trees stand tall along the beach, dancing to the breeze emanating from the sea's waters.

The sea grasps and sea oats gather in clusters next to the shore. Their coloured flowers are splendid and brighten with the shining of the summer sun. The sweet scent of the flower grapes sends a signal to the world of hope brought by nature.

The atmosphere is intensified by the aroma produced by the buoyant sea flowers.

In addition, from afar, images of leafless trees are also observed.

It mesmerizes the eyes to gaze at the beautiful creatures that hover all over the beach and within the deep-sea waters. There are beautiful birds that fly all over the dry shoreline and over the seawaters. Their coloured feathers brighten the sea with reflections of their exquisite appearance.

There are many varieties of birds. There are pelicans and seagulls. Pelicans have been seen hovering over the sand, singing sweet melodies that make the atmosphere at the beach vibrant. The seagulls are also flying over the seawaters in small groups. They spread their wings to cloak a soft shadow on the gentle water ripples.

Next to the shore, sea turtles seem to enjoy the summer heat from the sun. Their eggs are exposed on the sand by the children that play on the shoreline. Bees fly from one flower to another above the sea grapes. The humming of the bees, as they gather nectar from the sea flowers, attracts insect-eating birds.

Large crowds gather all over the seashore. These people come to enjoy themselves on the beach. In the sea, people of all ages and sexes are swimming and playing. The scorching heat from the summer sun is felt on the foreheads of all individuals.

It makes the people chill themselves in the calm waters of the sea. The children have seen playing beach ball on the shoreline. Some children are also pelting each other with sand on the coastline. There are also young boys climbing the tall palm trees to gather fruits.

Vendors are carrying ice creams and soft drinks all over the coastline.

Children collect shells for fun. In the built shades people are reading books, journals, and magazines.

But among all the beauty, plastic bags, food wrappers, beer bottles and cigarettes are piling up.

Out at sea, fishermen are casting large nets into the waters. Some of them are perching on the edge of the shore carrying rods in their hands. Their faces filled with hope and anticipation.

The deep waters of the sea produce a marvelous view for anyone who gazes out. The water slowly runs low on the shore. Small waves crash on the shoreline.

Deep out to sea, there are high waves that lift boats up and down mightily.

The beach can be perfect for views and activities. It is a place for everyone.

3. The Autumn

Many people dislike autumn, even though, it can be beautiful. They see it as being on the way to the wizardry winter, and the unknown darker world.

When the months go by, stories of goblins, myths of horrible creatures are told.

Schools can be back, but most people still head for the beach to see if the sand and the nice cool breeze are there.

The sea breezes lash around and make the barbecues sizzle. The warm smell of smoked beef, ham, and even turkey, is mouth-watering!

The days unfold slowly before the night of the disco galaxy. The stars glitter and gleam like diamonds.

People stay in their houses just because they dislike autumn.

Spring has its flowers. Summer, its sun, and even winter, the season that most people dislike, has its snowballing or skiing.

The September mornings are bright and airy. Horses and cattle munch and graze their way through the fields. The horses snort and toss their heads, glad to be alive. Then they break into a gallop, scaring the crows away.

Some early dark spots appear on some of the leaves.

There is an opera of bird song coming from the branches.

In the distance, you might hear a witch wail for joy. It's not that horrible.

For now, rivers flow joyfully between fishermen's legs. They stand motionless hoping to catch a plump juicy trout.

The mountains stand like giants, hovering above the teeny-looking houses.

4.The winter's Tale

Winter can be the most outstanding season, and much more fun than summer. Summer is just about being hot - so hot that you might want to peel off your skin.

But in winter, you only need to put on extra layers. The more, the better. Although too many can cause trouble.

A thick layer of white blankets covers the bare ground. Drops of icicles topple over each other like an upside bullfight.

Christmas is coming. Tales of fairies spread around. Stories are told of Santa Claus. We watch movies and snatch at popcorn. New students go to schools, and new uniforms are worn.

Christmas trees are cut, sold, then brought home by villagers. Decorations are hung. And we all wait for Santa by the chimney.

People go to church and listen to the melodies sung by children! The secret presents, made by elves who work for Santa, are wrapped. Then we all wait, wait for the night bells of a sleigh.

Glow sticks are spilled on PJs, making them glow by themselves.

Santa arrives, stuffing the stockings with precious toys like teddy bears. He leaves some nuts, or fruit.

Stories of hobgoblins and fairies are told and retold. They're hiding in their tiny, tidy leaf-made houses.

5. The wonderful Tilgate Park

Today, my online lesson suddenly crashed. So my mum and I went to Tilgate park to spend the morning

I saw many things in the park, many spectacular things.

The trees were bellowing in the flapping wind and the leaves were dancing on the branches. The hedge thorns were spiking as hard as possible. The daffodils were as yellow as the brightest marmalade sun.

The older trees were hooked like raincoats on a peg. The birds chirped above our heads, high above the lovely Tilgate park.

As a squirrel scurried away to climb a tree and get its nuts, a milky, pale swan flapped its wings noisily as it was chased by a small growling dog.

The green throated duck waddled from the lake to the weeds; it was both gorgeous and marvellous.

I walked past the creaking bridge and the flashing waterfall.

The crow's noise was like an alarming bell that sounded in the distance.

I saw a fully grown apple tree!

I touched the smooth surface of a small apple. I suddenly heard the train.

6. The race of nature

The dimming sun settled. Below the towering cliffs, Blyton stumbled across the bay. Fear engulfed every bone in her body. She had never felt so alone. A curtain of clouds swallowed the emerging pearl white moon.

Blyton was shivering. The stars in the sky winked sympathetically at her.

The dancing waves pirouetted in the angry squalls.

The crashing cliffs tumbled above me; I am about to run like an Olympian.

The waves waved to me. As the wind made the icicles dance on the branches, it was a chance of a lifetime. It was like a dream.

The flowing river that raced into the sea, was running ahead. My chance was going, and I had run before the crashing cliffs were going to erupt and start the race. I wouldn't let that happen. I will try my best to beat the modest player in the game.

As the marmalade sun blew the whistle, I started running to the finishing line... and I won.

I must try my best and win the competition. My award was to enjoy the natural world.

As soon as the flaming sun rose the next morning, I ran back sleepily to my bedroom. What a nice night, what a relaxing race. My god! It's almost 7 a.m.! I'd better hurry to sleep.

7. The Meadow, the plain, and the forest

Gracefully, the chirping grasshoppers skip as they dance around the meadow.

A brook babbled as lily-pads and the lotus flower flowed past. The Eden-green swamp shrunk, and the unending, brochure-blue sky dampened the moors. Du Maurier strolled across the Amazon-green plains.

The night had fallen; and Du Maurier still hadn't found her way home.

She walked past the azure lake, past the glinting stars of the night skies, past the misty fox holes, past the yolk-yellow ducklings, past the multicolored bouquets, past the pollen-rich smell of sunflowers. She then started walking towards the deep, dark, damp woodland when a large grumble came from the twig house. Canopy leaves were tied to the twigs and bamboos, while a huge rock hid it from view. Du Maurier explored the forest, and eventually found the house.

The roof had fallen in. Du Maurier moved inside and had a happy life.

About the author:

I was born in Hong Kong. But my dad's business is in China, so I grew up mostly in China.

I've enjoyed drawing for as long as I can remember. I listen to what my mom and dad say, and although I could not walk when I was eight months, I had a perfect control with a pen to draw. I still remember when I was three years old, my dream was to become an artist. After I was five years old, I changed my mind, and I wanted to be a fashion designer. When I was nine years old, I suddenly asked my mom, "Do you think I should be a fashion designer or an author?"

At that moment, I knew I had fallen in love with writing.

I went to study in the UK at the age of eight. Going to the UK to learn had a significant impact on me.

I want to thank Aunt Doris for inspiring me to love reading. She took me to a bookshop in Oxford when I went to the UK in April 2019 to take my Year Four interview exams.

Wow! This bookstore had a wide selection of children's books! It got my attention right away! My mom bought me all my favourite books. From then on, I fell crazily in love with reading. I even sometimes read my book when eating!

The year 2020 was going be crazy for coronavirus and destined to be remembered by all who lived through it. I was no exception.

My parents and I flew back to Hong Kong after school was closed in March 2020. I started writing my first story on my iPad while I quarantined at the hotel. Since then, I have been out of control.

I have been writing these stories off and on for almost a year. Then, suddenly, my mum found that I had written more than 30,000 words, and she thought she should keep it for me. And so, this book was finally printed!

Now, I'm already working on another novel of mine. It's an exciting story about a wizardry school.

Printed in Great Britain
by Amazon

74201918R00142